# The
# Floating
# Minyan

# The
# Floating
# Minyan
## of Pirate's Cove

The Adventures of
"EMES" Junior Interpol

based on the characters
created by Gershon Winkler

by

## Miriam Stark Zakon

Illustrated by
Sigmund Forst

The Judaica Press
New York
1986

# The
# Floating
# Minyan

# CHAPTER 1
## A Conversation In Miss Liberty

*I*t was a glorious summer day—a day of clear blue skies, radiant sunshine, and cool breezes. The kind of day New Yorkers dream about and see only a few times each year. The perfect day for sightseeing with a friend.

"Isn't she gorgeous!" exclaimed Simcha Goldman dreamily, as the ferry chugged closer to Liberty Island. "It really makes you think!"

"It makes me think how in the world she has been able to hold up her hand for so many years without getting tired!" his friend Moshe Tamari said with a laugh.

"Moshe, can't you ever be serious? That statue is a landmark. Years ago, when my great-grandparents came to America, they saw that statue and knew 'they'd made it!' It stands for something. And that's part of its beauty!"

He was right, Moshe had to agree, the statue was beautiful. They both were silent as the boat inched closer to the tall, majestic Statue of Liberty.

The ferry tooted its loud horn, its engines grew silent, and the passengers disembarked.

The two boys made their way towards the gigantic base of the green statue, joined the line outside, and, after a short wait, began the long climb up the stairs. As they trudged higher and higher, Moshe hummed a quiet tune. Simcha walked silently, his face pensive.

"A *shekel*[1] for your thoughts," Moshe said as they stood at the top of the statue, gazing down at the harbor and the panorama of New York City.

"Oh, I was just thinking how peaceful it is here," Simcha answered. "It's hard to imagine that not too long ago we were involved with terrorists and hostages and spies."[2]

"Simcha, even top notch sleuths like Emes Junior Interpol* need a vacation sometimes," Moshe said with a grin. "And who knows what can happen? Perhaps at this very moment, my father—" here Moshe felt a twinge of homesickness at the thought of his father, Colonel Tamari, an important official of the Shin-Bet, Israel's intelligence agency, ". . . is at a meeting somewhere, stuck with a problem, and thinking that only Emes Junior Interpol can solve it!"

"Fat chance!" Simcha snorted. Then he looked at his watch and gasped. "Say, if we want to make that show in the planetarium, we'd better make tracks!"

And, like tourists everywhere, the two rushed off, trying to cram ten hours of sightseeing into an eight-hour day.

---

[1] *shekel*—Israeli coin.

[2] For details of their exciting adventures, see *The Hostage Torah* by Gershon Winkler, and *The Egyptian Star,* by Miriam Stark Zakon, both published by The Judaica Press.

*Emes Junior Interpol is the name Moshe Tamari and Simcha Goldman made up for their detective team. Emes, which means truth in Hebrew was formed from the first letter of each of their first names (MS).

As they raced towards the waiting ferry, Simcha could not help but chuckle at the thought of the imaginary meeting in Tel Aviv which his friend Moshe had dreamed up.

# CHAPTER 2
## A Meeting In Tel Aviv

*I*n fact, just as Moshe Tamari had imagined there was a meeting going on. But the name of Emes Junior Interpol never came up. The meeting was taking place in a nondescript building in a somewhat shabby section of Tel Aviv.

In the lobby of this very building lounged an equally nondescript janitor. His name—Ariel Zohar, army veteran, crack marksman. And, incidentally, a respected member of the Shin-Bet.

Ariel turned to a short, wiry man who had entered only a few seconds before.

"*Shalom, Moshe,*" he said cheerfully as he rose from his seat. "Glad to see you. It's been a long day."

Moshe Weiss, a fellow member of the Shin-Bet and Ariel's replacement for the afternoon shift, looked sharply at his comrade.

"Anything wrong?" he asked quickly.

"No, no," Ariel reassured him. "Just meetings, nothing but meetings and more meetings." He paused. "This morning, though, there's a very special meeting."

Moshe's dark eyebrows shot up. "Special?" he asked.

"Still going on. The colonel and—"

"And—" prompted Moshe.

4

"And the Man."

Moshe's eyebrows shot up even higher, and seemed perilously close to leaving his head and soaring off into the sky. He whistled.

"Must be something big," he said.

"Keep a sharp eye out," Ariel warned. "And have a good day."

Ariel had hardly walked out the door, when Moshe heard footsteps outside the building. Keeping a close eye on the door from behind a large Hebrew newspaper, his body tensed up slightly—then relaxed as he observed a thin, grandmotherly woman bustle in.

"Moshe!" she cried out, with evident surprise. "Of all people! What are you doing here? Why, the last time I saw you—"

"Mustn't speak of that, Mrs. Stern," Moshe said with a laugh. "Though how you manage to always be on the spot when there's action, I'll never know."

"Just my *mazel*,[3] I suppose," Mrs. Stern said with a sly smile. "Can I see Colonel Tamari?"

"He's in a meeting now, but I'll take you up." Moshe stood up, walked to the tiny elevator, and pulled a small, harmless looking switch.

"Something new?" Mrs. Stern asked curiously.

"It announces your arrival," Moshe answered, "and it also jams the front door so that no one can come in while I'm escorting you."

"You've got a lot of new gadgets to play with, haven't you?"

"Wait until you see this new one," Moshe said, not without pride. He pulled the switch a second time, and the tiny window

---

[3] *mazel*—luck.

in the elevator began to glow. "Put your fingers there," he instructed the astonished older woman.

"What in the world for?" she demanded.

"Checks your fingerprints and automatically sends it to a central computer, which verifies your identity. If you are not who you say you are the elevator jams, an alarm goes on, and we've got you!"

Moments later the glow faded. "You check out," said Moshe with a laugh. "Not that I had any doubts. You are inimitable, Mrs. S.!"

"It was simpler in my day," Mrs. Stern mused, as they entered the small elevator. "You had a password, and that was that. Though I always managed to forget what it was!"

The elevator groaned and squeaked its way to the fifth floor. The door opened, and Moshe stuck his head out.

"She's okay, Ella," he shouted. Then, with a nod and a salute to Mrs. Stern, who'd already left the elevator, he pressed a button and the elevator door shut.

Mrs. Stern walked briskly down a small corridor, into an anteroom filled with cartons and steel filing cabinets. A young pretty woman sat at a desk in the corner.

"Shalom, you must be Ella. Shulamis Stern. You're new here, aren't you? I'm here to see Colonel Tamari."

"He's in a meeting now, *Giveret*.[4] If you'll just take a seat . . ."

"Don't worry, I don't mind talking to him when someone else is there. This is just a friendly visit."

"But—"

"No, no, don't get up, my dear. You've plenty to do, I'm sure, and I know my way in!"

Ella Drori had passed a battery of tests, physical and psycho-

[4] *Giveret*—Ma'am.

logical, before being given this particular job. She'd had intensive training and experienced instructors. Unfortunately, no one had prepared her for one such as Mrs. Stern. And so it was, that, seconds later, Mrs. Stern burst into the Colonel's office, followed by a frantic and dismayed Ella.

"Colonel," Ella gasped. "I'm so sorry. But this woman, she . . ."

Tamari, taken aback for a moment, saw who his uninvited visitor was and smiled at his secretary.

"Don't worry," he sighed in mock despair. "You can do a good many things, my dear, but no one expects you to stop a tornado singlehandedly. How are you, Shulamis?" he warmly asked the grinning woman.

"Thank G-d, thank G-d," Mrs. Stern answered. And then, to complete Ella's surprise she turned to the Man, the man whose presence turned the knees of veteran spies into jelly, and said breezily, "You're looking peaked, *Bubbale.*[5] If I would have known you'd be here, I would have brought some of my strudel!"

At this, Ella closed the door hurriedly behind her, lest her employer hear her burst into a highly unprofessional giggle.


One block away from this very ordinary building, guarded so well by such men as Ariel Zohar and Moshe Weiss, was another building, similarly uninteresting. Like many buildings in Tel Aviv, it had been undergoing renovation for some time. A scaffolding put up around its seventh floor had been up for over a year, not unusual in a country where frequent strikes were the rule and where a builder could run out of money and put off completion of a job until something "turned up." A cursory

---

[5] *Bubbale*—literally, little grandmother, or doll.

check by a sharp-eyed Shin-Bet agent, who had noticed the construction in the vicinity, had turned up nothing unusual.

On this bright, sunny and hot day, there were two construction workers on the scaffolding, lazily hammering at some wooden boards. Nothing seemed unusual, except that if one looked closely, behind a pile of cinder blocks, they'd see a dark, somewhat heavy, short man who had concealed himself and was staring intently through binoculars toward the fifth floor of the building parallel to his. The construction workers had been told by this man that he was part of a secret government operation. They had been paid well—too well for them to ask any questions. A secret government operation? Yes. But no one had thought to ask which government.

At the very moment that Mrs. Stern and Moshe Weiss were chatting and ascending in the elevator, this Russian gentleman, who was chosen by the KGB not so much for his brains, as for his amazing ability to read lips under difficult conditions, had his binoculars focused on the two men sitting in Colonel Tamari's office. His parents, still living in a small province outside Moscow, were both deaf, and had taught him as a child the art of lip-reading. Later, he'd applied this ability to languages other than Russian, and so, as he watched the lips of the two men, it was as if he could actually hear them speaking.

"So is he safe now?" the older man had queried.

"Perfectly safe. But, I think the chances of detection are less if he crosses no more borders right now."

"And the debriefing?"

"I'm sending an agent. Code name: Courier. I'm expecting Courier in my office momentarily, so that you two can meet."

"Will the debriefing take place immediately?"

"As soon as possible. He needs time to rest. He's over 70 years old, you know, and this has been quite an ordeal for him."

The swarthy man heard this exchange and smiled. At last! He was on the track. He pulled a handkerchief from his pocket wiped his sweating brow and then once again gazed intently at the window.

Suddenly he saw the door of Tamari's office open, and an older woman burst in.

"So that is Courier," he murmured to himself. "Ingenious! No one would have suspected!"

With a sigh of relief, Yuri, as the short, swarthy man was called, put down his binoculars. It was terribly hot up there, with the sun beating down upon him and the cinder blocks blocking any breeze which would have brought relief.

Well, he now knew who Courier was. All he had to do was wait for her by the corner, follow her to her destination and then cover himself with glory.

As his superiors had remarked several times before, Yuri had an incredible abilty to read lips in many languages, but he simply was not too smart.

Yuri climbed down from the scaffold, bid the preoccupied workers farewell and hurried to lie in wait for Courier. For Mrs. Stern.

Mrs. Stern turned her attention from the Man and spoke to Colonel Tamari.

"So what's new over here, Asher? I was in the neighborhood, some shopping, you know, and I said to myself, Shulamis you can't, you simply can't, pass right by without stopping in."

As Mrs. Stern chattered on, she almost unconsciously moved closer to Tamari's desk. She fingered a picture of Tamari's son Moshe which stood in one corner, and fondly asked about her young friend, now visiting in America. Then she brushed some dust off the desk, chiding Tamari for his sloppy housekeeping.

Tamari, who could not help grinning at Mrs. Stern's nonstop chatter, pulled one of the many files on his desk closer to him, hoping that Mrs. Stern would take no notice of his action.

No luck.

"What's that you're trying to hide from me?" demanded Mrs. Stern.

"Nothing! I'm only trying to clean up my desk, as you ordered."

"If it's nothing, why are you blushing like that? Let me see it." And, with the same zeal and determination which had defeated the young secretary earlier, she managed to grab hold of the blue folder.

With great surprise she looked at the name written on the front of the folder.

"Bar Eliav? Yehuda?"

Tamari glanced at the Man, sitting silently in his chair, and nodded, resigned.

"What's this about Yehuda?"

With another look at the Man, and after a slight moment of hesitation, Tamari began to explain.

"It's thirty-six years, Shulamis. Time to close up the file."

"Close the file? What do you mean?"

"What I said. Close the file. Declare him dead."

"Dead?? Close the file and forget him! How dare you!" Mrs. Stern turned indignantly to the Man. "Do you have any idea who this man was?"

"Of course I know of him," the Man replied soothingly. "He was a hero, a great hero."

"More than a hero," Mrs. Stern said, and then in a quieter tone, "He was a friend."

# CHAPTER 3
## Freedom Fighters

$T$he place—Palestine; the year—1948. This tiny country, the goal and hope of countless Jews throughout generations, was once again rocked by violence.

This was violence rooted in the past. Some two thousand years before the Jews were cast out of their homeland as their Temple blazed into ashes. This once fertile land, crying for its people, withered; the people themselves, crying for their land, learned the bitterness of exile and ghettoes and pogroms.

Then, with the beginning of the 20th century, the Jews began to return to their home. And the British, having obtained sway over the sacred land after the First World War, with the very help of the Jews themselves, did not know what to do. The aspirations of the Jews seemed fair and well-deserved; but what of the Arabs, whose leaders adamantly refused to concede even one inch of land?

In trying to please both the Arabs and the Jews, the British succeeded in satisfying neither.

In 1917 the British government issued the Balfour Declaration, indicating that "His Majesty's government looks favorably upon the establishment of a national Jewish homeland." Ecstasy among Jews; anger among Arabs.

Then, just as Hitler's fiery furnaces began to murder millions of Jews; just as the Jews of Europe desperately needed a place,

11

any place, to run; the British, acceding to Arab requests, slammed the gates to Palestine shut. The infamous White Paper, issued in 1939, severely limited Jewish immigration into Palestine. It meant an end to the hopes of millions of European Jews. It meant the end of the dream that a national homeland could be won peacefully.

And thus the violence began.

By 1947 World War II had been won, and the terrible results of the White Paper had become clear. With the smell of the gas chambers still in the air, the Jews' war against their former allies was in full swing. The enemy was the British; the battlefield—all of Palestine.

Three groups were involved in this battle for freedom. The largest was the Haganah, representing the majority of the Jews in Palestine, particularly those in the kibbutzim and border settlements. It was the Haganah which was to become, one year later, the basis for the army of the new State of Israel.

For quite a long time the Haganah had put its faith in British promises, in the possibility of negotiating a settlement. As far back as 1930, though, there were men who felt that the state could be won only by arms and violence. And thus was born a second group of freedom fighters, the Irgun Zvai Leumi, composed largely, of the city-dwelling Jews of Palestine.

The Irgun began its campaign of violence against the British much earlier than the Haganah. Like the Haganah, though, they stopped all activities against the British during the Second World War, realizing that their common foe, Germany, was a much more potent threat to the Jews.

The third group, Lochamei Cherut Yisroel (Lehi) was composed of former Irgun members who felt that the battle against the British was so urgent that not even the World War could bring a truce.

But, in 1948, all three groups were hotly fighting against British occupation and defying the White Paper by smuggling into Israel thousands of illegal immigrants who had survived the concentration camps of Germany and Europe.

This "illegal" immigration was perhaps the most heroic and poignant aspect of the struggle against the British. Here were thousands of Jews who'd managed almost miraculously to survive the war and Hitler's concentration camps. Now, when their only desire was for peace and a home to welcome them, they were denied this.

To reach Palestine most had to brave rickety, unsafe ships; frightening voyages; night landings on dark beaches in freezing water; and the possibility of being captured and sent to a detention camp in Cyprus. Yet they braved all these dangers to come to Palestine. Some were shot while trying to reach land, some drowned when their ships sank, some spent years behind barbed wire. But they came, determined to reach the only place in the world they could now call their home.

Both the Irgun and the Haganah took part in these "illegal" activities: buying ships, hiring captains and arranging mass escapes.

In early 1948, Yehuda Bar Eliav, a former partisan with the Russians, who himself had been an illegal immigrant in 1944 and who had joined the Irgun Zvai Leumi soon after his arrival, was sent to America. His goal—obtain two or three ships, so that still more Jews could be brought into their homeland. He also planned to buy arms for the impending War of Independence.

Bar Eliav had gone to America, to New York. A few weeks after arriving in New York, he'd vanished. And had never been seen or heard from again.

## The Challenge

"He's never been seen again," repeated Colonel Tamari wearily. "It's now thirty-six years that he's missing."

"Never seen, true, but you know quite as well as I do that he's been heard of."

"Rumors, nothing but rumors," Tamari retorted. "Someone reports seeing him in 1965 in London; then he's sighted in Istanbul in 1971, and in Paris in 1977. What do you think he is, some sort of ghost who turns up to haunt old Irgunists? The man is dead, I tell you!"

"And I tell you, there's no proof of it!" Mrs. Stern's voice turned low, dangerously low. "You must admit that his personal appearance was unusual, unique."

"Unusual?" For the first time, the Man spoke.

"Yes, unusual! Six foot five—a strong man, with jet black hair and a scar running down his face, from his eye to his lip."

"He got that during his days fighting Germans," Tamari interjected.

"A man of that demeanor has been sighted by reliable sources several times over the past thirty years. Why are you so anxious to declare him dead, anyway? Seems to me you never put much effort into finding him!"

Tamari was clearly at the end of his store of patience. At that moment Ella buzzed and hesitantly walked in.

"A man to see you, Colonel," she said. "Says he's a courier of some kind."

Tamari and the Man exchanged swift glances. "Tell him to wait one minute," he said with a nod of dismissal.

Then he quickly turned back to the angry Mrs. Stern. "Look, Shulamis, I've got work to do and I can't be bothered with this nonsense."

"So you refuse to reopen the inquiry?" Mrs. Stern asked.

"Absolutely. If you're so anxious to find him, find him yourself."

Mrs. Stern's eyes gleamed. "Maybe I will," she said defiantly.

Again, that swift glance between Tamari and the Man.

"It's a wild goose chase, Shulamis, and you'll get no help from this agency. None at all."

Mrs. Stern gazed calmly at the angry Tamari. Then her glance traveled over the room, resting for just one short moment upon the photograph of the young man which stood on Tamari's desk.

"Maybe I can do without your help, Asher. We shall see."

As the door closed behind her, the Man's face lost its nonchalant look, and lines of worry appeared on his forehead.

"Was that wise, daring her to find him?"

"Nothing said in anger is ever wise," Tamari answered glumly as he lit up a cigarette. "But now," he added, brightening, "let's talk to Courier."

# CHAPTER 4
## Sightseeing

"When, Simcha, when? I'm hungry and exhausted and just about to collapse."

"Just another block, Moshe. We cross the street over here. Hey—watch out for that cab. Look out!"

With barely inches to spare, Moshe jumped out of the path of a bright yellow taxicab which had sped through the intersection.

Moshe, startled by his close call, froze in the middle of the busy street for a moment. Immediately several drivers irately honked their horns.

Simcha grabbed his friend by the arm. "Come on, you one man traffic jam," he said. "It's right in here."

As they walked into a kosher delicatessen, Moshe said: "And I thought the Tel Aviv traffic was a mess!"

With hardly a word spoken between them the boys wolfed down corned beef sandwiches. Climbing that statue and all the other sightseeing they'd done sure had made them hungry! Then, hunger pangs allayed somewhat, they turned their attention to the french fries and began to talk.

"So when are we heading home, my friend?" Moshe asked. "All this subway riding has worn me down."

"Don't tell me you don't enjoy cramming yourself in a subway car with two million other people?" Simcha asked in mock surprise.

"Sure, a thrill a minute. Not to mention the army training I'm getting!"

"Huh?" murmured Simcha, his mouth too full of cole slaw to speak.

"Sure. After riding your IRT, I'm ready for a month on a submarine! And tank duty will seem easy!"

Both boys laughed and then dug into the eclairs they'd ordered for dessert.

After they'd both finished eating, Simcha remembered one more sight Moshe probably would like to see.

"Unless you're really tired, Moshe, I think it would be interesting to take a quick look around here. It's the diamond center of America and the world, too, I think. Here you can see a totally different breed of Jew. Chassidim. Many of them work around here. They're kind of odd, but interesting. They follow . . ."

"They follow the teachings of the Ba'al Shem Tov, who lived in the 1800's and stressed joy and dancing and prayer in G-d's service. And most of them follow a *Rebbe*,[6] who is kind of like their leader."

Simcha stared at his friend in astonishment. "Moshe, you amaze me, you really do! How'd you know so much about Chassidus?"

"Well," Moshe answered, rather shyly, "they've always rather interested me. I never knew a Chassid personally, but there are quite a lot in Israel, you know—especially in Jerusalem. I read up a bit about them, because they seemed so . . . well, so otherworldly and so dedicated to their ideals."

The boys paid their bill, left a tip for the waiter, and prepared to leave the coolness of the air conditioned restaurant behind.

[6] *Rebbe*—Rabbi.

"Dedicated and other worldly?" Simcha said almost cynically. "More like strange, it seems to me."

"Hey, Simcha, do I detect a note of dislike in your voice?"

"No . . . okay, yes. I do dislike them, I think. They've always seemed so clannish. And they look so odd, the way they're dressed."

"Clannish? Funny, that's just how I described you religious Jews before I met you, Simcha." Moshe opened the door and felt the heat blast into him. "Let's face it, my friend, in that skullcap and black suit, you don't exactly look like a typical American yourself."

With that, the two boys joined the teeming mass of people rushing down the busy street.

## An Answered Prayer

"Isn't it something!" Moshe said with a sigh, as he gazed at the bustling city far below them.

"Look, there's a helicopter! And we're higher than it is!" Simcha cried.

"It's gorgeous!" exclaimed Malka, Simcha's nine-year-old sister, who, after strenuous pleading, had been allowed to join her brother and his guest on their expedition to the Empire State Building.

The three gazed down at the city, at the unique Chrysler Building, the impressive United Nations, the Hudson and East Rivers and the grassy expanse which was Central Park.

"Simcha," Moshe said, after a time, "I'm sure having one terrific vacation!"

And he was, truly. When Simcha, who had been studying in a yeshiva in Israel, had invited his friend to join him for his upcoming visit to New York, Moshe had accepted eagerly. And he hadn't been disappointed, not at all! Although Moshe had already spent a year studying in New York on a previous visit, he hadn't had much time to wander through the city and enjoy its tumult, its excitement, its numerous landmarks and museums and sights.

But what was really astounding was how much Moshe enjoyed the hours spent in Simcha's local *Bet Midrash*.[7] Who would have thought that one could enjoy and actually revel in the massive Talmud books which lay open before each student? But the constant challenge, the arguing and clarifying were more rewarding, more exciting, than Moshe would ever have imagined.

"Yes," he mused quietly. "A great vacation. Almost perfect."

"Almost?" Malka asked. "Why almost?"

"Well," said Moshe, reluctant to appear as if he were complaining, "I'm just a little disappointed that I won't get to see more of America."

"Yes, so am I," Simcha agreed. The boys had wanted to leave the New York area, and travel to Disney World in Florida, or even California, but the Goldmans felt that they were too young to travel unchaperoned and so they had vetoed the idea.

"And one more thing," Moshe continued. "To tell you the truth, I was just a bit disappointed that this vacation has been so . . . so tame. No smugglers, no hostages, no mysteries," he added sheepishly.

"True. Seems that Emes Junior Interpol has been simply resting on its laurels."

The sun hid behind a cloud. The atmosphere became just a bit glum.

---

[7] *Bet Midrash*—synagogue and place of study.

"If you really want adventure," said Malka determinedly, "why not pray for it? G-d answers prayers, you know," she added seriously.

Moshe laughed. "We just put in our order for one full fledged mystery, is that it?"

"Yes! If you won't do it, I'll do it for you!" And she screwed up her face in concentration, looking so serious that the boys didn't have the heart to laugh at her.

"Do you want to go visit the museum here in the building?" Simcha asked, a few moments later.

"It's so incredible out here, I hate to leave," Moshe answered.

"Yes, it is breathtaking, isn't it?" a voice boomed out.

The three young people turned simultaneously.

"Mrs. Stern!" Moshe and Simcha shouted.

"One and the same!" the jovial woman said. "I called your mother and she told me I might find you here. Would you like to join me for lunch? There's a pizza shop close by—kosher, too," she added, with a glance at Simcha. "And I've got a proposition for you."

Simcha and Moshe looked at each other in anticipation and excitement. In their last adventure in Egypt, they'd found out that this full-time grandmother of twelve was also a part-time agent for the Israeli intelligence agency, the Shin-Bet. If Mrs. Stern was consulting with them, surely that meant adventure. Adventure . . . and mystery.

"Looks like Emes Junior Interpol is in business again," Simcha said to Moshe, quietly, lest Malka overhear.

Moshe, with a look at Simcha's younger sister, said to Mrs. Stern: "Mrs. Stern, I don't know if you're a fairy godmother or an angel, but you sure are the answer to our prayers! And pizza—that sounds terrific!"

### Encounter in New York

"A walking calamity!" Simcha thought to himself, as he glanced towards Mrs. Stern who was speaking to a police officer. "An accident looking for a place to happen!"

The three young people and Mrs. Stern were still together, but they were not, as might be expected, sharing a hot cheese pizza and a Coke. And, at the pace that the police questioning was going, it did not seem likely that they would soon do so.

Simcha, to pass the time, thought over the events of the last hour.

Simcha, Moshe, Malka, and Mrs. Stern had joined the dozens of other tourists in the crowded elevator which was to take them down from the top of the Empire State Building. In the last minute, as the doors were about to slide shut, a swarthy man with thick bushy eyebrows had placed his foot in the door, and somehow squeezed himself in.

"Room for one more," he'd muttered in an accented English, ignoring the glares of the already crowded passengers.

The man, restless it seemed, had tried to make his way towards their little group, and then changed his mind and turned away. In so doing, he'd managed to bump into Mrs. Stern's hand, and somehow the umbrella which invariably accompanied Mrs. Stern had opened.

The next few moments were a confused mixture of shouts, squirming, pushing and somewhat painful stabs of umbrella spokes, as Mrs. Stern tried vainly to disentangle and extricate herself from the mess of arms, legs, and umbrella which surrounded her. To compound the discomfort of the crowded passengers, everyone's ears began to pop as the elevator made its speedy descent.

When the elevator came to a stop and the doors opened, the man who'd caused all the trouble disappeared without even muttering an apology!

"What a city!" Moshe had exclaimed, as they walked into the street.

"And what a nasty man," Malka added.

"And what a mess," Mrs. Stern concluded, ruefully gazing at the ruins of her umbrella.

"Let's go to that pizza shop," Simcha had suggested, "I think we can all use a rest."

But, alas, it was not to be. They hadn't walked more than a block, through dizzying crowds of rushing people, when a tall young man bumped right into Mrs. Stern, and then careened on ahead.

"My purse! He's got my purse!" Mrs. Stern shouted, after a moment's startled pause.

Simcha and Moshe immediately gave chase, with Mrs. Stern panting behind them, trying to keep up. They wove through the masses of people, many of whom looked at them with irritation. At one point they came dangerously close to upsetting a cart of one of the many sidewalk peddlers jamming New York's streets. Into the street, inching around the stalled traffic, avoiding a speeding bicycle, ignoring the horns of impatient drivers . . . and then down, down the steps, two stairs at a time, into the stuffiness of a subway station. Too late! The purse snatcher placed a token inside the machine and disappeared into the doors of a waiting train while Simcha and Moshe watched, chagrined. They had no token themselves, and they hesitated to jump over the token machine, knowing full well that the token booth attendant would be after them in a moment, and by the time explanations would be given, the purse snatcher would long be gone.

The boys walked slowly back up into the sunshine. Mrs. Stern, who had just reached the subway stairs, looked questioningly at them.

"I'm sorry, Mrs. Stern," Moshe said. "He got away."

"So much for Emes Junior Interpol," Simcha managed a grin.

Mrs. Stern comforted them. "These fellows are professionals and have their escape routes all planned. The only thing to do is go to the police and report the robbery. But first," she nervously added, looking around, "we'd better find your little sister."

Malka! In the excitement of the chase the boys had forgotten all about her.

More concerned than he cared to show, Simcha wended his way through the never ending mass of people, looking this way and that. He tried, unsuccessfully, to mask the relief on his face when his sister came into view.

"Hey, kid," he said gruffly, "this here is one fast city. You've got to keep up."

But Malka ignored him, and with a look of obvious puzzlement on her face, turned to Mrs. Stern.

"Don't worry, dear, I'm all right," Mrs. Stern reassured her.

"I know this sounds crazy," the girl said, "but is it possible that someone is following you?"

"Me? What do you mean?"

"You know that man, the rude one, who started all the trouble in the elevator?" Malka said slowly. "Well, as soon as you took off after Simcha and Moshe, I saw a man come out from the doorway of a store, and run right after you! I'm sure it was the same man!"

Simcha and Moshe cast excited looks at each other. Mrs. Stern being followed! It could only mean great things to come.

But Mrs. Stern's astonishment rang true. "Following me? That's strange. Whatever for?"

She smiled kindly at Malka. "Don't worry, my dear, it's probably a coincidence. Or he may be one of those strange types whom you find in large cities, the kind who always wants to be where the action is. I'm sure no one is following me."

She patted Malka's hand reassuringly, and led them towards a policeman standing by a coffee shop to ask where the nearest police station was so that they could report the theft. But as she walked on ahead of them, Simcha heard her mutter quietly to herself: "Following me? Whatever for?"

"Well, that's it, kids." Mrs. Stern's voice broke through the clouds of Simcha's musings. "Luckily, I had my passport, credit cards and most of my traveler's checks in my knitting bag at the hotel. But I'd hoped to treat you to a nice meal—now it looks as if I'll have to beg carfare from you to get back to the hotel!"

"You've had such a hard day," Simcha said. "Why not join us for dinner at my parents' house? I'm sure they'd love to meet you."

"And we can take care of you and make sure nothing happens on the way!" added Moshe impishly.

Mrs. Stern agreed to the change in plans, and the four quickly left the police station where Mrs. Stern had just completed the report of the theft.

# CHAPTER 5
## The History of a Partisan

"*A* wonderful meal," Mrs. Stern smiled appreciatively at Simcha's mother, Mrs. Goldman. "And a wonderful family you have."

"Yes, we think we'll keep them," said Rabbi Goldman with a laugh.

"It's getting late . . ." Mrs. Stern looked significantly at her watch.

"Oh, you're not going back to your hotel at this hour!" exclaimed Mrs. Goldman. "Please stay the night. We've got plenty of room."

The boys joined Mrs. Goldman in urging their friend to stay. "It'll give us plenty of time to talk about our friends in Israel," Moshe said eagerly.

A light glowed in Mrs. Stern's eyes. "So it would, at that," she said. "Fine, thank you so much for the invitation."

Soon after dinner, Malka, exhausted by the day's activities, went up to bed. Mrs. Goldman excused herself, and went upstairs to dress for a meeting which she was to attend later that evening. Rabbi Goldman left the house, with a cordial "good-night," for his nightly ritual—an hour of study at a nearby *Bet Midrash* with a friend and *chevrusa*[8] of twenty years.

The boys and their friend were left alone in the living room.

---

[8] *chevrusa*—study partner.

25

"What's going on?" Simcha and Moshe asked together, eagerly. "Why are you being followed? And who are we after now?" Their questions, bottled up through the long day, came out in a rush.

"First of all, I don't think I'm being followed," Mrs. Stern said severely, restraining their enthusiasm. "Whatever for?" she repeated for the third time that day.

"But," she smiled at them, seeing their disappointed faces, "I do have a missing person for you. And finding him is not going to be easy. Thirty six years is a long time."

"Thirty six years!" exclaimed Simcha.

"That's right—1948. The year the mystery starts; the year the trail ends. Now, if you can contain your questions for a few minutes, I'll give you fellows a short lesson in history."

"Russia during World War II," she began, "was not a very nice place. Life in the Russian countryside, difficult even in the best of times, grew intolerable as the Nazis advanced. And for the Jews it became worse than intolerable—it became deadly.

"When the Nazi invasion of Russia advanced further into the country, many Russians, Jews and non-Jews alike, took to the Russian forests. Partisans, they were called. They fought a kind of guerrilla war—blowing up bridges, sabotaging military installations, doing whatever they could to make it harder for the Nazis to advance. They lived in small bands, often hunted like animals, scrounging for food and shelter and ammunition.

"The best of these partisans, by some accounts, was a fighter, a giant of a man, standing six feet five. His code name, Dagger—no one then knew his real name—and he made regional Nazi commanders tremble. He was shrewd, he was fast, he was fearless. Captured once, he'd managed to escape from under the Nazi eyes, returning with a nasty bayonet scar running from eye to lip as a souvenir of his prison stay. This was Dagger—the eighteen-year-old who led the Nazis on a cat-and-mouse game they were never to forget!"

"Eighteen years old?" Moshe exclaimed.

"Sssh!" Simcha reprimanded him. "Go on with the story, Mrs. Stern," he added, spellbound.

"Yes, eighteen years old. In war you grow up quickly, if you grow up at all. Particularly if you're a Jew.

"Yes, Dagger was a Jew, though few, if any, knew of his origin. But for some reason, a reason he never discussed, in early 1944 he began to urgently feel his Jewishness, and to feel that his place, now that the Nazi defeat seemed only a matter of time, was with Jews.

"He took a treacherous, almost impossible overland journey to Palestine. He had a talent for languages and he was quick-witted and daring, but still it has always seemed a miracle that he managed to do it. He reached Palestine in mid-1944, a hardened veteran at the age of nineteen, with a forged passport, a scar running the length of his face, and three Swiss francs in his pocket. Soon he became one of the top men in the Netanya branch of the Irgun.

"You've heard of the Irgun, haven't you?" Mrs. Stern asked.

"Of course," Moshe answered. "Why, my father was in it!"

"I know that you know," Mrs. Stern said, with a touch of impatience. "What about you, Simcha?"

"Yes, I read a bit about them. They were a terrorist organization in Israel before the state was formed."

"Terrorist, shmerrorist!" Mrs. Stern exclaimed. "We were freedom fighters! The British, whose unfair occupation of our country, whose immoral laws let millions of Jews perish in Europe while Palestine was closed to them, they may have called us terrorists! We were freedom fighters, just as George Washington was!"

"We?" Moshe queried. "Does that mean that you were an Irgunist, Mrs. Stern?"

Hard to think of this grandmotherly-looking old woman as a terrorist—freedom fighter, that is. Moshe's mind went back to their adventure in Egypt, and he remembered how she'd saved them from the hands of the kidnappers. Maybe not so hard to imagine, at that!

"Yes, I worked for the Irgun. And through my work with the Irgun I met Yehuda Bar Eliav, formerly known as Dagger."

"The partisan?" asked Simcha.

"That's right. His experience in Russia had made him a valuable fighter. The things he pulled off, right under the noses of the British! Unbelievable, what he could do. I was rather close to him, as close as anyone could get, for he was a very reserved person. He and I served as the "welcoming committee" for illegal immigrants for a while, helping them land on a beach near Netanya in complete darkness. Once, he rescued three young children, carried one in each arm and one around his neck, through the freezing water! He was something very special!"

Mrs. Stern grew silent, and her eyes seemed to gaze back at the past, as if it were unfolding before her.

"Well, what happened to him?" asked Moshe, as ever the impatient Israeli.

"When 1948 arrived, we realized that our old enemy, the British, would soon be gone. We'd gotten what we'd wanted! Only now we had a new enemy, the Arabs!"

"We needed arms, we needed ammunition. We needed ships to bring them in, and to bring in the masses of refugees waiting to enter *Eretz Yisroel*[9] as soon as the British left.

"Yehuda asked to be sent to America to help get arms. Normally a fighter of his caliber would have been kept for the field, but to tell the truth, Yehuda was sick and tired of fighting and killing. He believed in our cause, but he'd been fighting since he was a young boy, and he needed a break.

---

[9] *Eretz Yisroel*—the land of Israel.

"So Yehuda Bar Eliav went off to America to try and beg, borrow, or steal arms and ships. And this man, this Dagger, who'd survived Russia in the war, who'd made it to Palestine and eluded the British for years—he went to America and soon after his arrival, he was never heard of again. Disappeared, in mid-1948, without a trace!"

"Without a trace? Just disappeared?" Simcha asked, astonished by the story and its strange ending.

"Perhaps I shouldn't say without a trace. There were traces. hints, rumors that he was alive. He was a very unique looking man, as I said, standing six feet five, with jet black hair and sporting that scar! Not a man one would forget. A friend of mine, also an ex-Irgunist, swears he saw him in Paris, eating in a sidewalk cafe, some twenty years ago. My friend was on a passing bus, and by the time he could get off the bus, the man had gone. Then there was a bit of a mess in Istanbul in the early seventies, and a contact of mine from your father's office," with this she glanced at Moshe, "a contact told me that he recognized Yehuda's voice at a rendezvous in the dark."

"Rendezvous!" Moshe exclaimed. "I'd sure like to hear that story!"

"Ask your father one day," Mrs. Stern smiled. "But what I'm saying is, I think Yehuda is still alive, and I mean to find him."

The resolution in her voice seemed to waken Simcha from the dreamy mood which her story had evoked in him.

"One minute," he said slowly, "if Yehuda Bar Eliav is alive, why doesn't Colonel Tamari send men out to find him?"

Mrs. Stern hesitated. "He gave me the assignment—in a way," she said, suppressing a grin. "He told me to go and find him myself and to get my own help. That's why I'm contacting you boys. I'm too old to go running around this country by myself, and it's been so long since I've been here, I don't think I know my way around anymore. I need help. I need Emes Junior Interpol, as you call yourselves. Unless," she added mischievously, "you're afraid of the challenge."

"Of course not!" "No way!" came both boys' indignant protests.

"So you're with me?" asked Mrs. Stern.

"We sure are!" the two cried with enthusiasm.

"Only," Simcha added in a small voice, "where in the world do we start?"

# CHAPTER 6
## The Rebbe

"*W*here do we start?" Mrs. Stern repeated Simcha's query. "We start, naturally, at the beginning. Or, rather, at the end. The last known whereabouts of Yehuda Bar Eliav."

"Which were—" prompted Moshe.

"Brooklyn. Williamsburg, to be exact. A small Chassidic neighborhood, where members of a small sect of Chassidim who follow a man called the Rebbe live."

"Chassidim?" Simcha asked incredulously.

"That's right. Yehuda needed a cover when he first got to the States, so he took on the identity and passport of a Russian immigrant, a member of that particular sect, who was then living in Palestine and who was a supporter of the Irgun. Yehuda was supposed to come here in that identity, and then change names and roles and go on to make his contacts. But from what I understood from the letter I received before his disappearance, Yehuda was very impressed by the Rebbe, the Rabbi who headed that particular sect—"

"So we contact this Rebbe, and see if he has any leads for us," Moshe said eagerly, excited to finally be back in the mystery business. "It's a long shot, but you never know. Is he still alive? How do we get in touch with him?"

"That's where you come in, Simcha," Mrs. Stern said. "His is not a very well known branch of Chassidus, and I couldn't find out where he lives now, or if he's even still alive. But your father, with all of his yeshiva contacts . . ."

"My father knows very little about Chassidim!" Simcha protested.

"He might not know of the Rebbe personally," retorted Moshe, "but he'd know who to ask. Come on, Simcha, don't let prejudice get in the way of good detective work!"

"Prejudice? Who's prejudiced against whom?" Mrs. Stern looked accusingly at Simcha, who was feeling more and more uncomfortable.

"No one," he said gruffly. "Okay, I'll do it. But what do I tell him? The whole story?"

"Why not tell him that I'm looking for the Rebbe, who befriended an old crony of mine, whom I'd like to contact. No need to mention the Irgun connection or the mysterious disappearance."

The next morning Simcha put the question to his father. To his surprise, Rabbi Goldman actually knew the elderly man called the Rebbe!

"A man of monumental stature," said Rabbi Goldman. "He's an example of the finest of European Jewry, and brilliant too!"

"How do you know him?" Simcha questioned.

"I've only met him once, but I've known of him for a long time. When you're something really special, Simcha, people find you out, even if you're modest. What do you want with the Rebbe?"

When Simcha had told the story, with the omissions which they'd agreed upon, Rabbi Goldman smiled.

"The Rebbe is an old man, still living in Williamsburg. A friend of mine knows him well, and can probably make an appointment for Mrs. Stern to see him. You might want to go too—if Mrs. Stern doesn't mind—meeting with the Rebbe is an experience you shouldn't miss!''

After promising Simcha that he'd see to it that very day, Rabbi Goldman turned to leave. Simcha ran to tell his fellow conspirators the good news.

True to his word, Rabbi Goldman returned home that evening with the news that they had an appointment with the Rebbe for the very next day. And so it was that early the next morning Moshe, Simcha and their elderly companion found themselves walking through the streets of Williamsburg.

Moshe looked around him. It was certainly a bleak landscape around them. Old brownstone buildings were crowded together, laundry hanging from their rusty fire escapes—the only sign of habitation. On practically every block was an abandoned or burnt building. Many of the storefronts were empty, their faded signs waving crazily in the gusty breeze. A few of the signs, Moshe noticed, had been lettered in Yiddish as well as English.

They turned a corner and the three of them came to a startled stop.

"It's like another world!" Simcha gasped.

"More like a time warp," Moshe said.

It did seem that time and space had changed radically as they had walked. Here, too, were brownstone houses, but all were in good shape, shutters and gables newly painted, windows gleaming in the sun. The stores were open, their windows stocked with gaily colored merchandise. But the truly surprising sight were the people—nearly all were Chassidim, some milling around corners, some striding purposefully to unknown destinations, many strolling from one shop to the other.

Here were young men, with uneven beards and flourishing side-curls; old men with grey beards, black caftans, and white socks reaching to the knee; bright-cheeked children with tiny curls poking out of black velvet caps; women in calf-length dresses and bright kerchiefs pushing baby carriages; young ladies in fashionable blazers and skirts.

Moshe was glad that he'd followed his instincts and left his blue jeans at home. Still, he felt out of place, with the long, wavy hair of which he was usually so proud.

They were strange, he decided. Simcha was right. They looked clannish and unfriendly.

The impression of unfriendliness lasted for all of two minutes, until Simcha, having trouble finding the address, hesitantly approached two middle-aged Chassidic men.

"*Anschuldiks,*[10]" he said, in heavily accented Yiddish.

"Anything wrong?" the man replied in perfect English.

Simcha sighed in relief. "My Yiddish is pretty poor," he smiled. "We're looking for 2023 Hooper Street."

"Oh, the Rebbe. You're not too far. Go down there to the stop sign, make a right, then make another right by the butcher shop . . ." He paused. "No, maybe you should make a right by the bakery."

"Let them go with Lee Avenue, better," the other man interjected.

"No, that way is too confusing. You know what," he turned to the puzzled trio, "it's very simple, really, but you're sure to get lost. Come with me, and I'll take you. Shimon, you wait here for me." And without hesitation he began to walk towards the main street.

Clannish and unfriendly? Moshe thought. Uh-uh. He made a mental note to try and avoid judging a person by his clothing and appearance.

The man led them through the bustling streets, pointing out various shops and sights and synagogues along the way. Finally he halted before an old apartment house.

---

[10] *Anschuldiks*—Excuse me (Yiddish).

"The Rebbe lives in here, fourth floor," he said. "It's better if you have an appointment, though, or you might be in for a long wait. People come to him from all over the world, you know," he added proudly.

"Oh, we have an appointment," Moshe said. "It's for . . ." he glanced at his watch, "it's for . . . five minutes ago! Come on!"

With hurried thanks to the stranger, they rushed inside.

The dark brick apartment house which had been the Rebbe's home for so many years had no elevator. Simcha and Moshe raced up the four flights, with Mrs. Stern puffing her way behind them. The boys should have felt relieved when they finally reached the top, but for some reason they didn't.

"Nervous?" Moshe asked Simcha in a whisper, as they walked down the badly lit hallway, looking for the right door.

"Yes, a little," was his reply. "I'd sure rather be playing ball."

"Or studying Talmud," Moshe grinned.

They halted before a dark green door which bore a small black metal plate imprinted with the Rebbe's name.

"Well?" Simcha said. "Give a knock."

"Don't you know the rule—ladies first!"

They waited for Mrs. Stern to turn the corner and join them.

"Is anyone home?" she demanded.

"We . . . well, we decided to wait for you to knock," Simcha admitted sheepishly.

With a groan and a stifled grin, Mrs. Stern knocked. A tall, black-bearded young Chassid opened the door.

"We're here to see the Rebbe," Mrs. Stern said, not at all intimidated by the young man's demeanor. "We have an appointment."

Without a word, the Chassid turned and walked through the tiny anteroom, and through a doorway. The three of them looked at each other, shrugged, and followed. They made their way through a small, but immaculate kitchen, equipped with what looked to be terribly old fashioned appliances, and followed the Chassid into a study.

The walls were lined with plain wooden shelves piled high with books of every conceivable color and size. There were a few wooden chairs and, in one corner, a shabby lectern. Right in front of them, sitting behind a scratched mahogany desk, was the Rebbe.

He appeared, at first glance, to be just another elderly, grey-bearded, black-garbed Chassid. Then he looked up from the Hebrew book lying open before him and smiled.

And, for perhaps the first time, Simcha and Moshe fully understood the meaning of the word "charisma."

It was a magnetism, a charm which the old man possessed, impossible for the boys to describe, and just as difficult for them to ignore. His eyes gleamed with intelligence, but there was a kindness in them too; it seemed that he could look into the very depths of a person's heart, learn its secrets and troubles, and then do his best to solve them.

This, then, was the Rebbe.

When he spoke the impression of kindness and wisdom was heightened. His English, though heavily accented, was precise and easily understood.

"What can I do for you, my friends?" he asked.

"My name is Shulamis Stern, and I've come to you for some information."

"Information?" the Rebbe repeated quizzically. "Interesting. And these young men are . . ." The question hung in the air.

"Moshe Tamari," "Simcha Goldman." The boys spoke quietly, uneasily.

"Tamari and Goldman. An unusual combination. You're Israeli?"

"Yes, just visiting."

"Good, good. And you," he turned to Simcha, "your father

is Rabbi Goldman, and you are a yeshiva student, and you think that much of Chassidus is superstitious. Am I correct?"

"Yes, Rebbe, that is, no, of course not, I mean . . " Simcha began a garbled answer and blushed. His discomfort eased a bit, though, when the Rebbe gave him a kindly laugh and glance.

The venerable Rabbi turned back to the impatient woman before him. "Information is what you seek? What manner of information?"

"It's about a man," Mrs. Stern said slowly, forming her words with care. "A man whom the Rebbe was acquainted with many years ago. Yehuda Bar Eliav."

The Rebbe gave Mrs. Stern a shrewd and penetrating look, but said nothing.

When the silence grew awkward, Moshe, feeling that more explanations were necessary, began to speak.

"Mr. Bar Eliav was a friend of Mrs. Stern's, you see, and he's been missing for thirty-six years, and Mrs. Stern thinks he's alive and we want to find him!"

It sounded strange, and a little ridiculous, when blurted out in such a fashion, but the Rebbe didn't smile.

"Thirty-six years is it?" he mused, half to himself.

"That's right. He was last seen in 1948. You do remember him, don't you?" Mrs. Stern asked anxiously.

"Yehuda? Of course. A strange man, a unique man. A good, if troubled, Jew in his way." He turned his glance to Mrs. Stern. "Why?"

"Why?" she repeated, startled.

"That's right, why? Why are you searching for a man who is almost certainly dead?"

Mrs. Stern told the Rebbe of the rumors which had always circulated around Bar Eliav's appearances, but the Rebbe shrugged off her answer.

"Before I speak further of this, Mrs. Stern, I must know—

why? Not why you think he is alive, but why you concern yourself with this matter."

Mrs. Stern hesitated, then spoke. "We worked together, Yehuda and I. He was reserved and shy, but the most courageous person I'd ever met. I was his friend, Rebbe, and I'd like to find him again."

The Rebbe smiled. "His friend. And you, boys—why are you involving yourselves in this quest?"

Moshe thought for a moment. He hadn't given the matter much thought, but suddenly it came to him.

"He did a lot for our people, and it seems to me that he deserves to be found and helped, if he's alive, and remembered and honored, if he's not."

"Also," Simcha could not help but add, "solving mysteries is our specialty."

For the first time the Rebbe seemed taken aback. It was Mrs. Stern who gave him a quick synopsis of the adventures of Emes Junior Interpol.

"So, my young detectives," the Rebbe said, when she'd ended, "you, too, care about this mysterious Yehuda Bar Eliav? Well," he continued, slowly and heavily standing up from his chair, "perhaps it is time. Thirty-six years, it is—you know the significance of thirty-six, Simcha?"

"Sure. The Hebrew word *chai,* life, is equivalent in numbers to 18, so 36 means life, twice. But . . ."

"No buts. Everything is significant, and everything has a time. It is, perhaps, time for a second life for Yehuda Bar Eliav."

As he spoke, the Rebbe moved awkwardly towards the lectern. He opened a drawer in the base of the lectern, shuffled through some papers, and finally held a small, yellowed paper in his hand. It was a postcard.

The Rebbe handed it to Simcha. "Read it," he demanded.

"'Rebbe, I am alive. Do not grieve. It is better that no one know who I am, where I am, or what I once was. I've no friends to miss me, none but you. I think of you often. Yehuda.'"

"No friends to miss me," the Rebbe repeated softly. "Yehuda was wrong. He did, and he does, have friends. It is time for him to acknowledge them."

Mrs. Stern, never having expected her belief that Yehuda was alive to receive such solid corroboration, seemed stunned. "When did you get that?" she finally asked.

"It was 1965, Mrs. Stern. I kept it, for I felt that one day it would be of use. I thought of Yehuda often, you know, and prayed that he had found peace and wisdom. I waited for him to communicate again, but have heard nothing since."

"Look, Simcha!" Moshe cried, as he inspected the yellowed card. "The postmark—I can still just barely make it out—Pirate's Cove, Georgia, June 11, 1965!"

"Pirate's Cove, Georgia! Is there really such a place?" Simcha seemed dubious.

"Apparently there is, Simcha," the Rebbe said, with a twinkle in his eyes. "And," he continued, growing serious, "it is there, in Pirate's Cove, Georgia, that Yehuda Bar Eliav disappeared. It is there, then, that his friends must search for him."

"Does the Rebbe feel that we should search for him, then?" Mrs. Stern asked seriously.

"You are his friends. Seek him out. Help him."

Despite the solemnity of the moment, Moshe and Simcha could not help but exchange excited looks. It was Pirate's Cove, Georgia (the very name made them shiver with excitement!) for them!

The Rebbe turned to the boys, looking grave. "It will not be an easy road, nor a swift one. Go with *mazel,* be blessed."

The aged Rabbi walked slowly back to his desk, and turned

his eyes to the book which had remained open before him throughout the conversation. He began to read from it:

"'G-d reigns; let the earth rejoice and the many isles be happy.' I was studying this when you walked in. It is a sign, a good one. Go with luck and blessings."

Correctly understanding this to be a dismissal, the three walked out, ready to begin their search.

# CHAPTER 7
## A Telegram

$S$houting to be heard over the din of the subway train, Mrs. Stern and her two companions made their plans.

"Well, boys, are you with me? How'd you like a trip to Georgia?"

The boys enthusiastically nodded, but then Simcha grew sober.

"What about my parents?" he asked.

"What about them?" Mrs. Stern countered.

"We have already asked them if we could go travelling. We were thinking about visiting Disney World. But they said no."

"But that," retorted Mrs. Stern, "was before you had me to chaperone you. Besides," she added with a sly smile, "I can be very persuasive."

Mrs. Stern's confidence proved to be well-founded. They arrived at Simcha's home and after some persuading by Mrs. Stern and much pleading by the boys, Mrs. Goldman was prevailed upon to give permission for them to join Mrs. Stern on a trip to Georgia, to "look up an old friend." A phone call to Rabbi Goldman and all was complete—they were going to Pirate's Cove!

"But where the devil is it?" Mrs. Stern said.

"And how in the world do we get there?" added Moshe.

Simcha then proceeded to the telephone, trying to locate the tiny Georgian town. Four phone calls and several minutes later, he had the information.

"Pirate's Cove is a very small town on Georgia's coast. It would be difficult, almost impossible, to reach it by plane— we'd have to change planes three times. Our best bet is to take an overnight train to Jessup, Georgia, and then try to get a taxi or bus out. Pirate's Cove is about twenty miles from there."

"A sleeper! Wow!" Moshe, whose longest ride on a train had been the three hour Haifa to Jerusalem route, was excited.

"When does this train leave?" Mrs. Stern asked.

"The Amtrak agent said there's an afternoon train leaving tomorrow. I made reservations for two sleeper compartments. Now, all we have to do is go and pick up the tickets."

"Great!" exclaimed Mrs. Stern. "I knew I chose my partners well. Let's go right now to the station for the tickets. Then I'll go to my hotel and you boys can return here to pack."

The three excited travellers once again boarded the subway train for Manhattan. Simcha and Moshe could hardly believe their good luck in having become part of this adventure!

After they picked up their tickets, the boys walked Mrs. Stern to her hotel a few blocks from the train station.

They waited while she got her key from the desk and were just about to leave when Mrs. Stern turned to them white-faced. The hotel clerk had given her a telegram with her key.

"Is everything okay? What's happened?" Simcha asked anxiously.

Wordlessly, Mrs. Stern handed the telegram over to the boy. Simcha read it aloud.

"'Yosef wounded in Lebanon. Return home as soon as possible. Ahuva.'"

"Yosef. My grandson," Mrs. Stern said faintly, tears forming in her eyes. Then, collecting herself, she turned to the desk clerk. "Please get me a ticket to Israel on the first plane available. I must return home at once!"

## Yuri Takes A Break

If there was one thing in the largest city of the largest capitalist country in this world that Yuri Karnoven disliked, it was the subway. Noisy and dirty, crowded with weary and oppressed laborers, it made him nervous and irritable.

And, he reflected, in the past few days all he'd been doing was getting in and out of those horrible trains!

Following "Courier" to New York had posed no difficulties, but once she'd reached New York the spy had obviously taken leave of her senses! Spending most of her time in the company of teenage boys, walking through strange Jewish neighborhoods (where Yuri had been hard put to blend inconspicuously with the crowds) and getting her purse snatched on the streets of Manhattan! Were these the actions of a master spy, one entrusted with a most delicate mission?

For a few moments he was assailed by doubts. Perhaps he had erred . . . It would not be the first time, and his superiors would not be pleased. But then he cast his mind back upon the conversation which he'd seen so clearly. Yes, she most certainly was the spy, code name Courier—and she would lead him to his quarry. All of this running around perhaps was a mere ruse to throw enemies off her track.

Well, he thought grimly, it will not help with me.

He continued tracking the woman through the streets of New York. It wasn't difficult, not with so many people, so many cars to duck behind. He saw the woman and her two companions make their way to the large and modern Madison Square Garden, watched them disappear underground on an escalator.

Sprinting down the stairs he followed them and saw them walk over to a ticket counter in the underground Amtrak station.

"Wonderful," he muttered to himself. "Finally they are leaving this wretched city."

He positioned himself behind a large pillar, where he could easily see their mouths move. And so it was that he found out their destination—Pirate's Cove, Georgia, via the Silver Meteor train to Jessup, Georgia, leaving at 4:15 the next afternoon.

"Wonderful," he thought to himself. Now he was hot on their trail!

As the three walked out of the station, Yuri casually sauntered over to another ticket window.

"One ticket, please, from New York to Jessup, Georgia, on tomorrow's Silver Meteor."

"Yes, sir."

As he pocketed his ticket, he saw that his quarry had disappeared. No matter, he thought. Tomorrow, at 4:15 P.M., Courier would be on the Silver Meteor—and so would Yuri Karnoven.

In the meantime he could get some rest, and wash off the grime from those dusty subway cars!

Yuri Karnoven walked contentedly out into the sunshine.

## The Rebbe, Revisited

Gloom, like the humidity of that hot and grey day, lay heavy and thick on the Goldman household.

The family had just returned from Kennedy Airport, where they'd seen Mrs. Stern off on her return trip to Israel. Rabbi Goldman had insisted on driving the distraught grandmother to the airport for her evening flight. Although everyone had tried to seem hopeful and optimistic, each was terribly worried about Yosef, Mrs. Stern's nineteen-year-old grandchild, who lay wounded in a field hospital near Beirut.

The boys could also not help but feel sorry for themselves when they realized that their adventure had come to an end. At 4:15 P.M. tomorrow the Silver Meteor would roar out of Penn Station, and their compartments would be empty. Mrs. Stern had assured them, at the airport, that she would be back and they would continue the search, but that seemed a long way off now.

"Might as well go back and get a refund," Simcha said drearily. Mrs. Stern had given the boys her ticket and asked them to return all three to Amtrak.

"Maybe we should go and tell the Rebbe first," Moshe said. "Maybe he can help."

"Forget the whole thing, Moshe. Let's just go and return the tickets. The Rebbe can't help us."

"Even if he can't, we still should go and tell him what happened," Moshe protested. "He's interested too, you know. He himself said that he really liked Bar Eliav. We owe him that much."

"But we haven't even made an appointment."

"So what? Look, let's give it a try. If the Rebbe will see us, fine; if not, we'll go on to Manhattan and get rid of the tickets, and I won't bother you about it again. Fair enough?"

"Fair enough."

Early the next morning they once again found themselves among the oddly-clothed Chassidim in the tiny neighborhood. Once again they made their way to the old apartment house and up the four flights of stairs. Once again the door was opened by the silent young Chassid, who wordlessly motioned for them to follow.

"Friendly fellow, ain't he?" Simcha whispered to Moshe behind the Chassid's black-garbed back.

The Rebbe, smiling when they walked in, grew immediately somber after they told him the news. He asked for the name of the wounded boy and his mother so that he could pray for his speedy recovery.

"Where does this leave Yehuda?" he asked, after writing the names on a slip of paper.

"Nowhere," replied Moshe glumly. "We can't go without Mrs. Stern. Simcha's parents won't allow us to travel by ourselves!"

The Rebbe was silent for a few minutes and then his eyes strayed to the door.

"Have you told your parents the reason for this trip?" the Rebbe asked.

"Not exactly," Simcha reluctantly replied.

The Rebbe shook his head. "That is not good. A trip cannot be successful if it does not begin well. Simcha, please get your parents on the phone. I'll tell them the truth, and we will see what can be done."

A long conversation on the phone in Yiddish followed. Simcha, who understood some of the language, could follow what was going on, but Moshe was totally lost.

"He's telling my father about Yehuda, and how we wanted to try to find out what happened to him," Simcha muttered out of the side of his mouth to the obviously perplexed Moshe. "Now he's offered to provide a chaperone, someone whom the Rebbe thinks would benefit from the trip. He says they shouldn't worry, that there's no danger."

"Fantastic!" Moshe said with excitement. Perhaps they would travel after all!

A few more minutes and the Rebbe hung up the phone, turned to the boys and said: "Your father has agreed. I will provide a chaperone for you. He will meet you this afternoon at the train station."

The Rebbe grew very serious. "This is not a mere pleasure

trip, boys, remember that. Yehuda Bar Eliav deserves to be found. And I believe that you can find him. 'Let the earth rejoice and the many isles be happy'—don't forget this. It may be important. It was the sentence I was reading when you first came to see me with Mrs. Stern. Now, go—with my blessings.''

## The Chaperone

Manhattan's Pennsylvania Station was a busy place. Travellers and their well wishers sat on the benches in the large waiting room, many impatiently glancing at the large board which announced what train was ready to depart. Constant announcements blared over the loudspeaker—"Last call for the 4 P.M. Metroliner, making stops at Newark, Trenton, Philadelphia, Wilmington, Capitol Beltway and Washington; All Aboooooooard!''—adding to the din.

Rabbi Goldman impatiently looked at his watch. "It's almost four and your train has been boarding for ten minutes. What can be keeping him?''

"I hope he'll show up," Simcha said nervously.

"He will. The Rebbe said he would," Moshe reassured him.

Five minutes passed, and then ten minutes. The Silver Meteor would be departing at 4:15, only five minutes from then. The question was—would the boys be on it?

Suddenly a large, sepulchural figure clad in black walked towards them.

With a start, Simcha and Moshe recognized the Chassid as the silent young man who had escorted them through the Rebbe's home.

"I am here. Are you ready?" he asked in an almost mournful tone.

"Ready?" Simcha shouted. His anxiety was rapidly turning to anger. "We've been waiting for you for almost an hour!''

"You've been sent by the Rebbe?" Rabbi Goldman asked the young man.

The black hat bobbed up and down in assent.

"Then hurry, or you'll miss the train!"

With hasty goodbyes the three went racing down the steps to the platform. Only moments after they'd rushed onto the train there was a long and melancholy blow on the horn and the Silver Meteor chugged out of Penn Station, bound for Georgia.

The three sat in one corner of the train, so that their benches would face one another. Then, with tickets checked and luggage stowed on the top railing, Simcha turned to the Chassid and spoke, trying his best to contain his anger.

"Why did you arrive so late? Two more minutes and we'd have missed the train!"

"It is as the Rebbe of Sadagora has said," the Chassid said solemnly.

"Huh?"

"The blessed Rebbe of Sadagora told his disciples: 'We can learn from everything, even from technology.'

"'What can we learn from a telegraph?' his Chassid asked him.

"'That we are charged for every word.'

"'And a telephone?'

"'That what we say here is heard there.'

"'And a train?'

"'That in one second, we can miss everything.'"

With this, the Chassid lapsed into silence, and Moshe and Simcha looked at each other, chagrined. What manner of man had the Rebbe foisted on them?

After a few moments of uneasy silence, the Chassid relaxed a little.

"My name is Shlomo Hersh. The Rebbe sent me to accompany you. And," with a glance at Simcha, "I'm sorry that I was late."

"Did your parents give you trouble about coming?" Moshe asked.

"I have no parents."

"Oh. I'm sorry." Moshe did not know what else to say.

The train pulled in and then out of the Newark station, while the boys sat in uncomfortable silence.

Simcha tried again.

"Shlomo, do you have any idea why the Rebbe sent you to be with us?" he asked.

"The Rebbe has been like a father to me," the young man answered. "All that he asks of me, I do." His words seemed to come slowly and with difficulty as if he wasn't used to speaking. "The Rebbe told me that I should come with you—that perhaps I could learn from you."

"From us?" Simcha was astounded.

"He said that I could learn from you much about friendship."

The Chassid said this quietly, almost sadly.

Simcha suddenly felt a little guilty. Here was a person, a fellow Jew, an orphan, apparently, whom the Rebbe had sent for them to befriend, and he'd had nothing but angry words for him.

"Sure, Shlomo," he said, in an attempt at heartiness. "I think we can be friends—if we work at it a bit." He stretched out his hand, and, somewhat reluctantly, the Chassid took it.

"How old are you, Shlomo?" Moshe asked curiously.

"Nineteen."

Only nineteen! The beard and grave demeanor made him seem much older.

"Speaking of friends," Simcha said, "did the Rebbe tell you about Yehuda Bar Eliav?"

"He told me nothing."

The boys then told their strange companion the entire tale of the mysterious Yehuda Bar Eliav. Shlomo, for his part, remained silent, but seemed interested.

When they had finished the young man excused himself and went for a drink of water.

When they were alone, the two leading members of Emes Junior Interpol looked at each other.

"Well?" Moshe asked.

"Well, if he goes easy on the Chassidic stories, and learns to smile a bit, I might be able to tolerate him," Simcha said.

"And maybe even like him," Moshe added thoughtfully.

# CHAPTER 8
## Sleepless Nights

The Silver Meteor made its speedy way over the endless miles of track which spanned the eastern coast. Baltimore, Richmond, Selma . . . the names flashed by and were forgotten. Georgia grew closer and closer.

In the tiny sleeper compartment, which consisted of nothing more than two short beds suspended from the wall, one on top of the other, and a small mirror, Moshe was restless. His was the top bunk, and although he could have strapped himself in, he liked to move around in his sleep and so he had not done so. Now with every curve or bump he felt himself fly over the small mattress. Twice, he'd found himself right by the edge, ready to topple over.

He opened the curtain on the window by his bed. It was a dark but clear night and he could just make out the Big Dipper. It must be about midnight, he thought to himself. Midnight—when strange things abound, and pirates attack, and people disappear. Yehuda, the Dagger, disappeared, among the pirates . . .

He slept, an uneasy sleep, full of strange dreams.

Not all passengers on the Silver Meteor were lucky enough to have sleeping compartments. Some, mostly for reasons of economy, were obliged to spend the night in their coach seats.

For Yuri, though, it was not a matter of economics. He had merely neglected to reserve a sleeping compartment. So he found himself trying to doze off in his chair.

It wasn't easy. Not with the thoughts which were revolving through his head.

Failure. I am a failure. I had Courier, I had her. She said that she would be on this train, the Silver Meteor. That cunning woman! She had it all planned, down to the last detail. She had even sent those two blasted boys as decoys. So here I am—riding to Georgia, following two boys and a bearded man who's joined them—but no Courier. No Courier, and no glory, and no success.

Maybe I should just get off at the next stop and go somewhere where at least I can get a decent night's rest. What then? Tell the Boss I failed? That, while I sat in this train, Courier escaped me? No, impossible. Better to continue and follow those boys. Perhaps they will still lead me to what I want. One never knows.

If they do, there will be glory and honor and vacations! Perhaps a *dacha*[11] outside of Moscow, lovely for winter vacations, with snow and skating parties . . .

He slept, a smile on his lips, and dreamt of winter in Moscow.

Midnight on the Silver Meteor is 7 in the morning in Tel Aviv.

"Seven in the morning! It can't be!"

Colonel Tamari took another look at his bedside clock, confirmed that it was, indeed, that late, and jumped out of bed.

Like most Israelis, Colonel Tamari was normally an early riser. But he'd had a sleepless night and had just fallen asleep, it seemed to him, a few moments before the alarm had woken him.

It was only yesterday morning that he'd seen Shulamis Stern's

[11] *dacha*—house (Russian).

grandson's name on the list of those wounded in a guerrilla attack. Shulamis might be difficult at times, but she was a good friend. Tamari, concerned, had immediately gone up to the Rambam Hospital in Haifa, where the badly wounded were transferred as soon as it was safe to move them.

He had spoken to Mrs. Stern. Though Yosef was badly injured, he'd come safely out of his coma, and the doctors were hoping for a full recovery.

Those fears set to rest, Tamari had conversed with his friend and part-time colleague, and soon found himself beset by new anxieties.

"Do you remember that conversation we had in your office, not long before I left to America?" Mrs. Stern had asked.

He remembered it well.

"Well, Asher I think I'm on the track!" She told of her visit to the Rebbe, and the mysterious postcard.

Tamari, to her surprise, did not seem pleased.

"I told you, Shulamis, that file is closed," he said curtly.

"That is not what you told me!" she retorted. "You said I could do what I wanted. That I could find my own help. And I did," she smiled, though she felt a bit uneasy. She wasn't certain that Tamari would be pleased when she mentioned his son's involvement, but she felt that it should be brought to his attention.

"You did? Who?"

"Emes Junior Interpol. You've heard of them, perhaps!"

Mrs. Stern was unprepared for the explosion which followed.

"The boys! You brought them into this too! Are you out of your mind?"

"What's the big deal? You yourself said it was a dead end! It is a dead end, isn't it, Asher?" she asked suspiciously.

"Yes, yes, of course." He waved her off.

"In any case, Yosef's wound ended our investigation. The

boys returned the train tickets. Our investigation, I'm afraid, will have to wait until my grandson is well."

Tamari's anger disappeared. "Let's hope Yosef is well soon, Shula," he said. "Now, I've got to get back to the office. Let me know if there's anything you need."

As soon as he had taken his leave, his anger and anxiety returned. He knew his son and his son's friend. He did not want them involved. Not now.

Thus, as Moshe Tamari wrestled with his thoughts and his uncomfortable mattress on Amtrak's Silver Meteor, his father, Colonel Asher Tamari wrestled with fatigue and anxiety in his Tel Aviv apartment.

It was, for many, a sleepless night.

## Spy Tales

The sun was just rising over the horizon, sending glorious lines of purple and orange across the sky, when the Silver Meteor departed from the Savannah station.

Conductor Bill Brode was oblivious to the spectacular pageant of color taking place outside of his window. He'd seen it often enough. Instead, he glanced at his watch, consulted a list and began to knock discreetly at certain doors in the sleeping car.

"We'll be in Jessup in twenty minutes," he called out quietly, opening the compartment door for a short moment.

Inside one cramped compartment Moshe groaned, rolled over, and found himself in mid-air. With a terrific bang he was on the floor, laughing, groaning, wide awake.

Simcha, after having made certain that his friend wasn't hurt, joined in the laughter. Perhaps it was the fact that neither had slept much, or the sheer excitement of sharing an adventure once again—whatever the reason, the two found themselves laughing harder and harder, unable to control their guffaws. A few minutes later, when Shlomo knocked lightly and walked into the small compartment, he found the two friends prone on the floor, still laughing. Tears rolled down Simcha's cheeks, and Moshe, doubled over in laughter, held onto his stomach.

Shlomo looked at the pair and then asked, puzzled: "What's so funny?"

"M-M-Moshe," Simcha gasped. "He fell off the bed!"

The young man's puzzlement grew greater. "What's so funny about that?" he demanded.

The laughter ceased. "What's so funny about that?" Simcha said. "I don't know, Moshe, do you?"

He caught his friend's eye, and the two of them burst into laughter again. It was only the conductor's voice, warning them that they were due in the Jessup station in ten minutes, which brought them back under control. Hastily, and with only a few giggles, they dressed and repacked their suitcases.

The Jessup station was quite small and few passengers got off with the three boys. When Simcha asked the lone ticket seller how they could get to Pirate's Cove, he was told, in a pronounced Southern drawl, that they'd need to take a taxi.

"Is there a number we can call for a taxi, then?" Moshe asked.

"Y'all wouldn't want to wake up ol' Abner, would you?" the ticket seller asked. "He'll be here around 'bout half hour, mo' o' less. Why not wait fo' him here?"

Recognizing that there was no way to hurry ol' Abner into appearing, the three sat down to wait. It was Moshe who suggested that they say their morning prayers and eat right there in the small station.

"But what about a *minyan?*"[12] protested Shlomo.

---

[12] *minyan*—ten Jewish men over age thirteen constitute a minyan.

"A *minyan?* In Pirate's Cove, Georgia! Come on, now!" said Moshe.

With a sigh, Shlomo opened his *siddur*.[13] Moshe and Simcha followed his lead, pulling *siddurim* and *tefillin*[14] from their bags.

After their prayers, Simcha opened the bag of food his mother had packed and shared with Moshe and Shlomo some cereal and evaporated milk. They were just ending their breakfast when an old green pickup truck pulled up to the front entrance.

"Hey, Abner," the ticket seller called. "Yo' got yo'self some passengers."

"Hop in, boys!" ol' Abner cried from his pickup truck, his eyes fixed for a few moments on Shlomo's black Chassidic clothes.

It is difficult, under the best of circumstances, to "hop in" to the back of a pickup truck, and, loaded down with luggage, it was almost impossible. Somehow, though, they managed to scramble up. The three settled themselves on a wooden bench on the side of the truck, and, having asked their driver to take them to Pirate's Cove, ("in one piece, please," Simcha had muttered) they sat down to enjoy the ride.

Which they did. Although it was early morning it was already quite hot. The road ol' Abner took was quiet, edged on both sides with green woods rich with the smell of pine and honeysuckle. The smells and the green scenery were such a contrast to the grey of New York that they all rode along in silence, absorbing everything.

After a few minutes, Shlomo broke the silence. "I'm curious," he said, "what made you both get involved in detective work?"

Moshe grinned. "It's in my blood, I guess," he said. "My

[13] *siddur*—prayer book.

[14] *tefillin*—phylacteries. These are worn by religious Jewish males over age thirteen during weekday morning prayers.

father is a colonel in the Shin-Bet, Israel's intelligence agency."

The usual reaction when he told others of his father's line of business—surprise and, in many cases, envy—was not forthcoming. Instead, Shlomo snorted.

"Spies! Oy, vay, what a thing for a Jew to do!"

The pause that followed was awkward as Moshe and Simcha both fought to contain their sharp retorts.

"You're wrong," Simcha finally said. "It's a fine thing for a person to be involved in. There can be nothing better, I think, than a Jew helping to protect his fellow Jews and defend *Eretz Yisrael!*"

Moshe looked gratefully at Simcha. He felt better, having his friend stand up for him. Poor Shlomo, he thought, a friendless person who didn't even know how to speak civilly to others! No wonder the Rebbe had sent him away!

"You know, Shlomo," Moshe said slowly, still feeling sorry for the young man, "Jews have been spies for the longest time. Even in the *Torah!*"[15]

"That's right," Simcha backed him up. "Joshua sent spies to Canaan, to check out the city of Jericho before they conquered it. Or have you forgotten that incident?"

"Yeah, and even Jacob, when he went to Egypt, made each of his sons enter Egypt through a different gate, so that they would not stand out! Now, that's a smart intelligence maneuver, I can tell you!"

"Yes, Emes Junior Interpol has roots that go way, way back!" Simcha said. Both of them laughed and Shlomo, after a moment, laughed with them.

"You know, I must admit that you're right," conceded Shlomo. "I'm sorry, Moshe, I shouldn't have said what I did. I guess I'm not used to talking to people much."

[15] *Torah*—the Five Books of Moses.

"No problem, Shlomo," Moshe replied. "After all, you got us to think and you got us to laugh. What's a friend for, if not that?"

"Yes, what's a friend for?" the young man said quietly. And all three lapsed into a convivial silence, watching the lovely scenery pass by.

# CHAPTER 9

## Confrontation in Pirate's Cove

$T$he sun rose in the sky, and it grew hotter, the air more humid and full of dust. And still ol' Abner and his pickup slowly rolled on.

In the back, sitting on top of their luggage, the three boys began to feel restless and uncomfortable.

"It's going to be a hot one today," Moshe remarked, wiping his brow.

"The air, it's so heavy," Simcha agreed.

"Will we ever get there?" Shlomo muttered, reflecting his companions' thoughts.

Finally, when they thought they could bear no more of the heat and the bumpy road, a small sign indicated that Pirate's Cove, population 890, was two miles ahead.

Minutes later the pickup ground to a halt. They were on Main Street, the only business street, it seemed, of the small town.

Abner came around to help them with their luggage. As he lent a hand to Shlomo to help him climb out, he peered closely at him.

"Hey, boy," he drawled, "yo' must be one of the Jews we done heard about!"

Simcha and Moshe exchanged swift looks. Was the monster of anti-Semitism about to rear its ugly head?

It certainly seemed that way. The three boys paid their driver, picked up their luggage, and slowly, uncertainly, made their way up the dusty street. On both sides of the street, in front of the small shops, groups of men lounged on old wooden benches. The three felt terribly conspicuous as the eyes of all of the men followed their slow progress.

"That's them," they heard one older man say.

"The Jews," another nodded sagely.

Sweat dropped from the boys' faces. Moshe clenched his hands tighter around the handle of his suitcase, his body tensed and prepared to fend off attack. Simcha tried to remember the karate moves he'd studied last year in a self-defense class, and at the same time began to mutter a *Psalm* to himself. Only Shlomo seemed perfectly calm, humming a Chassidic melody to himself over and over and over.

All seemed silent in the tiny town. The men on the benches had grown quiet and simply stared at the newcomers. Only the Chassid's humming broke the stillness.

Before them, walking towards them, the boys could see three figures. As they grew nearer, they realized that the middle one, a balding man of gigantic stature and and even bigger belly, was in a uniform of some sort. Two pistols hung conspicuously on a belt.

The three adventurers, unsure of what to do, continued walking. And slowly, the three men walked towards them, the distance between the two groups lessening, the menacing atmosphere intensifying.

The boys halted. The men, likewise, came to a stop. Only inches separated the two groups.

The uniformed man rested his hand lightly on his pistol for a

moment, then he drew his hand up slowly, ever so slowly . . .
. . . and grabbed Simcha's hand in a mighty handshake.

"Hi'ya son. Glad you could make it. We've been mighty worried about you," he said, a huge smile on his face.

## The Smuggler's Minyan

An elderly man standing next to the uniformed man smiled at the three bewildered youths.

"*Shalom aleichem,*"[16] he said, shaking their hands heartily. "Come and have a soda! There's still plenty of time."

"Plenty of time?" queried Moshe. "Time for what? How did you know that we were coming?"

"Of course we knew. We're the ones who sent for you. I'm Jake Gruen," the elderly man added, as if in full explanation.

"Sent for us? What do you mean, sent for us?" Simcha blurted.

"Why don't—hey, aren't you the fellows we sent for from Savannah?" the man who introduced himself as Jake Gruen asked.

"No, sir," Simcha replied. "We just came down to . . . to . . . to look for someone," he ended lamely.

"Hoo-whee! Talk about coincidence!" the uniformed man laughed heartily.

"There is no such thing as coincidence," Shlomo Hersh said gravely.

Mr. Gruen gave him a sharp glance, then smiled. "Maybe not, fella. But why don't you all come and join us for a cold drink, and we'll let you know what's been goin' on round here."

The uniformed man led the puzzled trio to a nearby bench which stood before a small cafe. He ordered Cokes for each of them and began to speak.

[16] *Shalom Aleichem*—welcome.

"So you boys don't know nothin' about Pirate's Cove, or why we've been waitin' for you, huh?" he asked.

All three shook their heads.

"Well, Jake, supposin' you enlighten them some," he said.

"Sure. I told you boys, I'm Jake. This here's Sheriff Bob Parker, and my friend here—" he pointed to a tall, thin man of indeterminate age and shy grin, "—he's Abie Connor. President of our local synagogue."

The boys stared at him open-mouthed. "Synagogue? Here in Pirate's Cove?" Simcha exclaimed, astonished.

"Sure! You mean you boys don't know about the Smuggler's Synagogue?"

"The Smuggler's Synagogue?" Simcha's astonishment grew by leaps and bounds.

"Well, it looks like you don't know much about our town," Jake Gruen grinned. "Let me start way back, at the very beginning."

"Pirate's Cove," the man lectured, "started back, must be three centuries ago. This is a coast town, you know, and all along this coast are harbors, inlets and coves—places where an experienced sea captain can guide a ship away from pursuers, places where someone inexperienced can wreck on a reef or rock. A perfect place for seafarers or outlaws running away from government ships. So centuries ago Pirate's Cove was built—and populated by outlaws, by—"

"By pirates!" interrupted Moshe excitedly.

"Well, not exactly, leastways there were only one or two of the Blackbeard type. No, it wasn't pirates, it was smugglers. Men who didn't like government interference. Some were criminals, some were innocent men impressed into a brutal Navy, some just good businessmen running rum into the country. Anyone who was running away from the government was welcomed, so long as they didn't bother anyone else. Together with the deserters, the criminals, the adventurers, came, every once in a while, the Jews."

"Jews?" Shlomo asked incredulously.

"Yup. Jews running away from governments who persecuted them, Jews who couldn't go anywhere else. A few might have been smugglers, but most were honest men and women persecuted because of their religion. They wound up here. Most went their ways, but a few would stay around. And like all Jews, they started a synagogue. The Smuggler's Minyan, it got to be called. Meets on holidays and for funerals and weddings."

"Did you say 'meets'?" Moshe asked. "You mean it's still around?"

Here Sheriff Parker broke in. "Hasn't missed a Yom Kippur service for 150 years!"

"Though it doesn't look too good for number 151," Abie Connor remarked glumly.

"That's not the boys' concern," the Sheriff said to him. He turned to the three young men, who were still too astonished to speak. "But you fellas will want to know why we kind of expected you."

"Yes, we sure would," Simcha replied.

"You see, lately the number of Jews here in Pirate's Cove has gotten smaller and smaller, and last year, when old Ike Cohen died, we lost our *minyan* entirely. Josh Berger moved to Jessup and little Willie went—well, you won't be interested in all this, but to put it simply, the Smuggler's Minyan needs Jews! Now, whenever we need a *minyan* we have to import Jewish men from Savannah."

"Brung them up from Savannah for Yom Kippur," Jake explained. "Now it's just a year that old Ike Cohen—"

"My best friend," the sheriff interrupted.

"Old Ike Cohen," Jake continued, ignoring the sheriff, "he passed on one year ago tomorrow."

"And Ikey had always asked that we have someone say *kaddish*[17] for him on his, on his—what was that word again, anyway?" The Sheriff turned to Abie, scratching his head.

"On his *yahrzeit*," Abie offered. "The anniversary of his death."

"Since you need a *minyan* to say *kaddish*," Jake continued, "we phoned the synagogue up in Savannah and asked them to send us Jews. Four of them. So when you fellas showed up, of course we thought . . ."

"That we were the Jews from Savannah!" Simcha said. "Well, we're not whom you expected, but we're Jews and we're all past *Bar Mitzvah*—will we do for your *minyan?*"

"Sure will!" Jake smiled.

"Hold on a minute," Moshe said. "Didn't you say you needed four Jews?"

"That's right," Abie answered. "We got six of us here in the Cove. Four more makes ten—the Smuggler's Minyan."

"But there are only three of us," Shlomo said slowly. "So where does that leave us?"

"It leaves us exactly where we were before you boys came," the sheriff laughed. "Waitin' for those Jews from Savannah."

"The whole town's lookin' for them," Jake commented. "Ol' Ike was a popular fella, and everybody wants to do right by him and his last wishes."

"That explains the reception we got!" Moshe said thoughtfully. "What a surprise!"

"There's one more train, due in about three hours," the sheriff said as he looked at his watch. "I sure hope those dudes will be on it."

"And I hope the train will make it through," Abie said dolefully. He sniffed. "Smells like hurricane weather to me."

---

[17] *kaddish*—prayer said on the anniversary of a person's death.

"Oh, Abie, you'd smell a hurricane on the moon!" Jake laughed. "We're just due for a hot spell, is all." He turned to the boys. "Now, maybe you want to look around Pirate's Cove a bit. See our synagogue and all."

"Sure!" all three said nearly simultaneously.

The sheriff was looking at the three of them curiously. "You ain't mentioned what brings you to these parts," he said mildly.

Moshe glanced at Simcha who, as if in answer to his mute inquiry, silently nodded.

"It's like this," Moshe began self consciously, "We're looking for someone who . . . who seems to have lived in Pirate's Cove. At least, that's the last we heard from him. His name's Bar Eliav, Yehuda Bar Eliav. He was here a while back—in 1965."

The sheriff whistled. "That's sure a while ago, boy. I've been here since I was a half pint and I don't recollect no one by that name. But I'll see what I can do about finding out about him— check the local records, that sort of thing."

"Yeah, and we can ask Charlie Murrow," Jake said helpfully. "He remembers everything and everybody. And Doc also."

"Sure, boys, we'll be glad to help," the sheriff said.

Simcha and Moshe smiled gratefully at the men. They hadn't thought that their job would be as easy as this! Then again, who would ever have thought that they'd be joining a *minyan* in Pirate's Cove, Georgia—a smuggler's *minyan*, at that.

"We've got quite a wait for the next train," Jake said. "You boys come with me now and I'll give you that tour of the synagogue."

The three jumped up quickly and followed their new-found friend down the dusty main street of Pirate's Cove. In the short time that they'd been speaking on the bench, the sun had grown much hotter, the air was thick with heat and filled with dust. The sky, which had seemed so blue in Abner's pickup, had streaks of pink and yellow in it now—lovely, yet ominous in the steaming heat. Simcha couldn't help but wonder if the pessimistic Abie wasn't correct in his gloomy assessment of the weather.

Shaking off a slight feeling of foreboding, he began to listen to Jake's words. The talkative Jake was pointing out places of interest to his fascinated guests.

"That there was Mobley's Saloon and Hospital. Closed some thirty years ago, after a fight over a baseball team wrecked the place."

"A saloon and a hospital together?" Moshe inquired in disbelief.

"Sure. Poured alcohol into the wound and also down your throat. One way or the other you recovered!" Jake laughed, a short, guttural sound. "Pirate's Cove was a pretty rough place in the old days. We've settled down quite a bit now. Just a lot of old characters now, folks like me, who don't want to act too civilized. Still, we've got laws, and a sheriff, and all that, just like other folks."

They continued walking, but their pace was slow, since every few minutes Jake would stop and either point out another part of Pirate's Cove or speak with one of the numerous old men who seemed to make up the town's population.

Although most of the people wore the same type of clothes as Jake—denim overalls and the oddest assortment of caps or hats that the boys had ever seen—they did notice one middle-aged man in a light summer business suit, complete with tie and cufflinks. But when Jake saw the man, he stepped off the curb and slowly made his way to the other side of the street. He kept his gaze carefully turned away from the well-dressed gentleman.

"Did you know that man?" inquire Simcha, curious about Jake's obvious attempt to avoid the middle-aged man.

"Wish I didn't," Jake answered briefly, some resentment evident in his voice. "Jem Fry. Banker in Jessup." And he lapsed into an uncharacteristic silence which puzzled the boys.

But a few minutes later, he was once again the talkative man of earlier, his silence and resentment gone.

Before they left the Main Street, Jake brought them to a small hotel—the only one in Pirate's Cove, in fact. They checked in and left their bags in the room. Then they continued on their guided tour.

The main street, it turned out, was only a few blocks from the water. They could now see the inlets and frightening cliffs and rocks which had been the bane of so many government ships years before.

For a few minutes more they walked, past piers and warehouses and countless small boats moored to the docks. The water was a beautiful shimmery blue and, except for the shrieking of the sea gulls, all was quiet.

"There was a time, during and right after World War II, when these here docks were used for fairly large ships. The other port cities were full of Navy ships, I guess. Now, no one uses it but us locals, and some city folks who come here for the summer."

"Isn't the synagogue in the center of the town?" Shlomo asked. He'd seen enough of ships and boats. He was sweaty from the strong sun and impatient to see the synagogue.

"Well, not exactly in the center of town," Jake laughed. "As a matter of fact, you're looking at it!"

All three turned their heads towards the direction in which Jake was pointing. All they saw was an old wooden pier, with a houseboat moored to it!

"But where? . . ." Moshe began.

"Right there." Jake once again pointed to the houseboat. "Don't you see? Just look at the name painted on her."

Amazed, the three boys walked closer to the houseboat. It was painted red, but weather had dulled the color to a kind of dull brown. Its trim was white and underneath a small porthole, in blue paint, they could make out faint markings. 'The Smuggler's Minyan' it said. Underneath was a small Star of David.

It finally dawned on them what they were looking at. "A houseboat," Simcha whispered. "You *daven*[18] on a houseboat!"

"Why not?" Jake said proudly. "The Rabbi who started it said it's okay by Jewish law, so long as it's tied down tight. It's kind of fitting, here in a place like Pirate's Cove!"

"Beautiful," Shlomo murmured, much to his companion's astonishment. They didn't see much beauty in the weatherbeaten old boat.

Sensing their puzzlement, he explained. "No matter where Jews are, they stay connected with their tradition. A *minyan* in a houseboat! In a town in the middle of nowhere! That's beautiful!"

Jake cleared his throat. "Not exactly the middle of nowhere," he corrected severely. Then, with a chuckle, he added: "The end of nowhere!"

"You know, it is kind of beautiful," Moshe had to agree, after he thought about it. "May we take a look inside?"

"Sure."

They made their way back up the pier carefully, noting as they walked that many of the planks seemed loose and rotten. The tide was low, so they had no problem jumping off the pier and onto the small deck.

"Follow me," Jake said, as he crouched and disappeared into the houseboat.

The boys, bending low, walked through the small doorway and into the cool dimness of the synagogue. And a synagogue it was, without a doubt, though it was unlike any *"shtiebel"*[19] which Shlomo or Simcha had ever seen.

[18] *daven*—pray.
[19] *shtiebel*—small one room Eastern European-style synagogue.

Benches lined the walls, in the style of *Sephardic*[20] synagogues. On one side was a small wooden closet, its weathered planks covered by an immaculately clean, white velvet curtain. The Tablets—symbol of the *Torah* for so many generations—had been sketched upon it.

"It's beautiful," Moshe exclaimed in awe. Simcha and Shlomo both spontaneously murmured verses from *Psalms,* instinctively feeling that they were in a house of learning and prayer.

Jake seemed pleased by their reactions. He did not interrupt their thoughts, but waited quietly in a corner of the room. After a few moments he gestured towards a doorway which was almost hidden. He passed through and the others followed.

"This here's the kitchen," Jake announced, somewhat unnecessarily, since cooking utensils and a small Bunsen burner announced the room's function. "Through there," he pointed towards another door, "is the dining room, where we all like to set a spell and eat, after a funeral or holiday service."

"It's just incredible!" cried Simcha, and Moshe nodded in agreement. For his part, Shlomo seemed dazed. "A *minyan* here!" he said, half to himself. "Who would have believed it?"

"A hundred and fifty years is a long time," Moshe said.

"Too bad we won't last much longer," Jake said gloomily.

"Why not?" "What's wrong?" all three piped up at once.

"That fella you seen, all dressed up. The banker. Seems he's found some papers showin' that his great-great grandpappy owned this boat and the pier, too. He let the synagogue use it, but never gave up ownership."

"Does that mean that he's Jewish too?" Simcha inquired.

"Yup. Not that he'd admit it. Changed his name to Fry, 'cause Freund seemed too Jewish for him. And now he wants to

[20] *Sephardic*—Jews descended from Spain and Portugal are Sephardim.

take over the old boat, build up the pier, and turn it into a restaurant for the summer people. Selling lobster, no less! It's hard to keep kosher down here in the Cove, but catch me eatin' lobster! My daddy would turn over in his grave, he would! Anyway, this Fry wants to make some money and he says you can't stand in the way of progress. Progress! Ask me, he just hates all Jews, 'cause he's one and don't want to be one!"

"Could he really do what he wants?" Moshe was appalled.

"Looks like it. We had a lawyer check the papers out. So far it seems they're okay. But that's not you boys' problem, it's ours. Now," he said, with a forced laugh, "suppose we start to look for this, this Eliav fellow."

The four of them walked out of the houseboat. Before they left the pier they turned back for a last look at the synagogue on the sea. And the same thought took root in the minds of Simcha, of Shlomo, and Moshe.

"Somehow, we've got to save it!"

## A Meeting With the Banker

As they made their way back to town they noticed a change in the weather. A day that had begun so lovely had grown steaming and oppressive; the sky was now multi-hued and threatening.

Simcha and Moshe saw another change, too, since they'd stepped into Pirate's Cove that morning. It was in their companion, Shlomo. The young Chassid, who had seemed so quiet and shy had somehow assumed the mantle of leadership. The synagogue on the houseboat had stirred his imagination, and the thought of it ending up as a lobster restaurant angered him immensely.

"We've got to do something about it!" he cried to his two companions.

Jake had left them off in town, assuring them that he could be located in an instant if they needed him. He'd pointed out some locals who might be able to assist them in their search for their missing friend, and invited them to return to the synagogue for the evening service when, hopefully, the Savannah contingent would have arrived. Then, with a cheery wave and farewell, he'd left them on their own.

Before Simcha and Moshe could begin to make a plan of action, Shlomo demanded that they put off their search for Bar Eliav for just a little while longer in order to save the synagogue, whose future was in immediate jeopardy.

"But what can we do?" protested Simcha, who nevertheless felt moved by Shlomo's words.

"Do? Let's go talk to that banker, Mr. Fry, that's what we can do. Maybe we can get him to listen to us!"

Objections a-plenty arose in Simcha's mind—the banker had no doubt been cajoled and pleaded with already; how can you reason with someone whose interest lies only in money and in "progress"; and why would he listen to three young kids anyway? But before he could voice any of these arguments, Shlomo was off, asking everyone in the street where he could find Jem Fry. It was all Moshe and Simcha could do merely to keep up with their suddenly energetic friend.

Shlomo hurried down the street, turned left, and raced up a driveway which led to a large, weathered, but lovely wooden house.

"This should be Fry's summer place," he explained to his two panting friends. Before they could talk him out of it, he'd rung the bell. After a short time, the middle-aged man that they had seen on the street opened the door.

"Hello, Mr. Fry. My name is Shlomo Hersh, and I'd like to speak with you. It's important." Somehow he made his way past the astonished banker, and was halfway into the living room. Moshe and Simcha could only follow.

"Yes?" The banker had finally found his voice.

"The *minyan*, Mr. Fry. The houseboat. You musn't do what you're planning. It's a sin, a terrible thing. That *minyan* has lasted for a century and a half—how can you, a Jew, destroy it? How can you take such responsibility? How can you take away someone else's tradition? If you don't believe in it, that's your loss—but why take away from the people in this town this wonderful houseboat synagogue—it has kept the Jews here together for over 150 years!"

"Now look here, young man—"

"Look, Mr. Fry. We three came to Pirate's Cove, by chance, to look for someone. But we found, nearly the moment we arrived, that the synagogue was in trouble. Coincidence? Impossible! We were sent here—sent to save that synagogue, that last remnant of Jewish tradition in this place. Wipe that out and nothing will be left!"

The banker's anger was obvious. "That is as it should be, young man. Your Judaism was fine for the ghettoes of Europe. Perhaps it's still fine in the State of Israel—but it has no place in twentieth century America! The Smuggler's Minyan will be renovated as planned. My decision is final. Now, please leave my home."

"No, Dad, let him stay. Let's at least hear him out."

All three turned quickly to the doorway, where a young handsome man of about twenty stood. The banker's gaze, so full of anger a moment ago, softened. The affection which he felt for his son was obvious in his look and in his abrupt acquiescence to his son's request.

"Okay, okay, Bobby. Come in then, young men." He motioned to a couch in a corner of the luxuriously furnished room and the three sat down. The banker seated himself in a leather recliner, while his son remained standing in the doorway.

Jem Fry's tone was milder as he addressed the black-garbed Chassid. "My son wants to hear your arguments. Please continue."

For a long moment Shlomo remained silent and Moshe and Simcha wondered if he'd grown timid. But then he began to speak, in a quiet, almost sing-song tone.

"We Chassidim," he said, "often like to retell stories and tales told by our Chassidic Rebbes. Perhaps, then, one of the Rebbes can speak better than I. Rabbi Mendel of Rymanov used to tell this tale:

"'There once was a peasant who had a calf which he wished to sell. He showed it to a noble, who asked him how much he wanted for his dog. The peasant, of course, insisted that the animal was a calf. After some argument the noble struck the peasant and said: "This is so that you remember, when a noble says it is a dog, it is a dog."

"'Some time later the noble's manor burned down. Disguised as an architect, the peasant came to speak to the noble of rebuilding. Taking him alone to the woods in order to inspect trees which were to be used for rebuilding, the peasant tied the noble around one of the trees and beat him soundly.

"'Just so you remember,' he told him, 'that when a peasant says it is a calf, it is a calf.'

"'The noble, terribly upset by this experience, grew ill. Some time later, he heard of a miracle healer who could cure him. The healer, who was actually this same canny peasant, came and instructed the noble's servants to leave him alone with their master. "This cure works best if the patient screams loud," he cautioned them. "Therefore do not interfere, no matter what you hear."

" 'The servants, trained to be obedient, ignored their master's screams as the peasant beat him again. "This is the second lesson," he told him. "When a peasant says it is a calf, it is a calf!" '

" 'The peasant then walked out, leaving the noble ill and furious.

" 'Some time later the peasant told a friend of his to go to the noble, whisper the words "It was a calf" to him, and then run away as fast as he could. The friend did so and the noble, certain that this was the peasant who'd inflicted such damage upon him, shouted to his servants to pursue the man.

" 'The shrewd peasant then came to the noble, who'd been left alone by all his servants, and beat him a third time. "Now perhaps you will remember," he said, "if a peasant says it is a calf, it *is* a calf!" '

"The Rabbi of Rymanov would end his story: 'The peasant was the angel Michael, guardian of the Jews. The noble was Sammael, the Satan himself. And the calf's name—the calf's name was Israel!' "

Shlomo paused for an instant, took a deep breath, and continued: "Just because you call something progress, and make fun of Judaism, does not make it so. A dog remains a dog; a calf remains a calf. If you insist otherwise you, too, will eventually learn the lesson—if a peasant says it is a calf, it is a calf!"

With this, Shlomo sat down.

After a moment's silence, Jem Fry cleared his throat and spoke. "Look, young fellow, that was a very . . . a very affecting story. But really, much as it might pain me, I simply cannot change my position. There's too much money and planning involved in all this. You don't realize all the ramifications, all of the effects of abandoning a project. No, I can't do it."

The banker stood up, indicating that he'd given the boys enough time. Slowly, with a deep sigh, Shlomo stood, followed by Moshe and Simcha. Shlomo paused for a moment before the banker, sighed again, and walked towards the door.

The banker's son, who had stood, silent, all through the narrative, walked out with them.

"My name is Bobby Fry," he said, his voice gentle and apologetic. "Sorry about that. That was some story."

"But it served no purpose," Shlomo said sadly. With nods to the young man, the three of them slowly walked back towards town.

# CHAPTER 10
## Jonathan Doar

$T$he atmosphere in The Smuggler's Minyan was as gloomy as a pirate's frown.

Four older Pirate's Cove men, the two members of Emes Junior Interpol, and one bearded Chassid all sat within the cramped confines of the synagogue-on-the-sea. From outside, they could hear the waves lapping against the weathered boards of the houseboat.

The eighth member of the *minyan*, Doc Stein, was expected momentarily, while the ninth, Jake Gruen, had gone to the Jessup train station to try and find out what was keeping the afternoon train. As yet, there had been no train, no Savannah Jews, and no *minyan*.

Suddenly the sound of feet scrambling unsteadily on deck was heard. All of the people inside craned their necks to see who it was entering.

"It's only Doc," one of them said, in obvious disappointment.

"Nice to have such a reception!" the elderly newcomer boomed out in a deep bass voice.

Simcha, Moshe and Shlomo looked at the man without too much interest. It had been an afternoon of disappointments. After their unsuccessful plea to the banker, they'd tried to follow up leads in the case of the missing Israeli, but none had panned out. Despite the cordial assistance of the sheriff in looking through the

77

town's old records, they'd found no trace of the elusive Mr. Bar Eliav. In addition, long talks with the town's elderly population had elicited no information. At the end of the long, hot afternoon they were no closer to finding Yehuda Bar Eliav than they'd been in New York! Further, a new problem—the nagging difficulty of saving this fascinating monument to Jewish faith, seemed unsolvable.

Shlomo had suggested that the *minyan* be moved to new quarters—the sheriff's office, perhaps—but his suggestion had been discarded by the old-timers, who felt that without its houseboat the *minyan* would simply die out for lack of interest.

So here they were—no missing person, no *minyan*.

"We haven't yet spoken to this new man," Moshe said to Simcha.

"Might as well try it," Simcha replied. "Though I doubt we'll get anywhere."

They approached Doc Stein, who had comfortably settled on a large portion of wooden bench. He seemed to know exactly who they were. News, it appeared, travelled fast in Pirate's Cove.

"Well, boys," he roared, "I hear you've been looking for a fellow by the name of Elion."

"Eliav," Moshe corrected mechanically. "Bar Eliav."

"Eliav, Elion. Don't know either of them. Sorry."

"That's okay," Simcha said, not bothering to hide his discouragement. "We really didn't expect you to."

"I simply can't understand it," Simcha continued, half to himself. "How can a person just disappear into thin air?"

"Particularly someone as tall as Eliav," Moshe laughed. "I mean, you can't very well hide six feet five inches under a bed."

"Six feet five inches, you say?" Doc seemed interested. "That's mighty unusual." He paused for a moment, lost in thought, and then turned back to Simcha. "This Elion fellow—what did he look like, exactly?"

"He was tall, as I said, six feet five inches. And he had jet black hair and a scar running—"

"—running down his face, from his eyebrow to his mouth. Right?" Doc said triumphantly to the startled boys.

"Right!" Moshe shouted. "Does that mean that you knew Bar Eliav?"

"Never heard of him," Doc answered. "But the person you've described sounds a lot like a fellow I once knew. Jonathan Doar was his name. I met him first in 1948, I believe. He lived in Jessup and spent summers up here in the Cove until, oh, must be 1965."

"Nineteen sixty five," Simcha murmured, lost in thought for a moment. Then he exclaimed, "The year the postcard was sent!" In mounting excitement he turned to the doctor. "Tell me, do you know where this Doar was from, what he did?"

"Well, he didn't speak much about his past. I wasn't too close with him. Met him in '48. He was brought into Mobley's, his head split open. Mild concussion I treated him for. He was a close-mouthed fellow, even after he recovered. He was a foreigner, I think, had some sort of accent, but I couldn't place it. Down here in the Cove if a person don't want to give answers, we don't ask no questions. He had a shack here in the Cove and came up with his wife for summers."

Simcha turned excitedly to Moshe. "It must be him!" he said. "The dates are right and the accent . . . I think we've found Bar Eliav!"

"It does sound promising," Moshe agreed. "Doc, do you know what happened to him since 1965?"

"As I'd said, he started a business, which did really well. Settled down, married a girl from Atlanta. Never had kids as far as I knew. Then, in '65, maybe '66, he upped and left Jessup and Pirate's Cove. Went north, I think. I don't know whereabouts. Maybe the sheriff could help you there. He was right friendly with Doar."

"The sheriff? But he couldn't help us before." Moshe was disappointed. Would the trail end here, in Pirate's Cove, in 1965?

"Don't you see, Moshe, you were asking about Yehuda Bar Eliav," Shlomo retorted. "Did you ever describe him to the sheriff?"

"No, I didn't," Moshe admitted suddenly feeling foolish that he neglected to do so. "Do you think he might—"

"Only one way to be sure," Simcha said, standing up. "Let's go and ask him."

"But what about the *minyan?*" protested Shlomo.

"It's too early to *daven ma'ariv* anyway. We'll be back before nightfall. Besides, Jake's not back yet. Maybe we'll meet him in town and find out what's going on."

After a hurried explanation, and a promise to return within the hour, the three young men quickly left the houseboat, jumped over the ever-mounting waves that washed on deck from the rising tide and raced down the pier towards the town, hot on the thirty-six-year-old trail of Yehuda Bar Eliav!

Sheriff Parker was quick to assist them in their search. "Doar? Jonathan? Sure I knew him. Close-mouthed fellow, but clever and loyal. Why didn't you say that was who you wanted?" He looked at them sharply. "I thought you guys wanted someone named Bar Eliav!"

"We have reason to believe that they might be one and the same," Moshe said seriously, sounding in his own ears like a television detective.

"Reason to believe, huh?" The sheriff looked at them shrewdly, and suddenly the boys realized that he might not be quite as slow-witted as he appeared. "Well, you fellows seem okay, so I won't give you a hard time asking a lot of questions. In Pirate's Cove, a man's business is his own." Another shrewd glance, a

---

[21] *ma'ariv*—evening prayers.

pause, and then he continued. "Last I heard, Doar had moved to a small island off the coast of Maine. It was called—what was it?—oh, yeah, Art's Island. It was a few miles off Portland. Like I said, he was a close-mouthed son of a gun who liked his privacy. He planned to run his business from there, he told me."

"Art's Island, off the coast of Maine," Simcha repeated. He looked at his Israeli friend and smiled. "Looks like you're going to get the travel you wanted, Moshe."

"But we can't leave now," Shlomo cried. "The *minyan* needs us!"

"Don't worry," Simcha hastened to calm the young man down. "We'll stay tonight and tomorrow if they need us. We couldn't leave now even if we wanted to, we've probably missed the last train out! We'll be here for the *minyan*."

"Ain't gonna be no *minyan*." It was Jake Gruen, who had quietly slipped into the sheriff's office.

"Jake? What's the matter?" Simcha asked, seeing the man's dejected face.

"Just what I said. Those fellows from Savannah can't make it here tonight. Seems they've had a spell of bad weather up Savannah way, and they were afraid to leave. Maybe they'll be here tomorrow, maybe not."

Jake looked somberly at Sheriff Parker. "Hurricanes," he answered shortly. "They think it'll pass us by, but who knows."

Hurricanes! The word sent a chill down Simcha's spine and Shlomo shivered. Only Moshe, not familiar with the word, seemed unaffected.

"Hurricane? Is that some kind of storm?" he asked.

"Storm? I guess you can say that. But they can get pretty rough, and can cause a lot of damage, particularly near the water."

"Yes, let's hope it passes us by. They usually do," Jake said. "Now let's go and tell the others the bad news."

"You mean there really won't be a *minyan* for *kaddish?*" Moshe asked. "Even though there are nine of us?"

"You know nine aren't enough. Got to have ten, or it don't count. But I do feel kind've bad about it. Old Ike was such a good guy."

"I can't believe this!" Shlomo exclaimed, much to the others' surprise. "This man, like every Jew, deserves a *kaddish*. And I'm going to see to it that he gets it!"

Jake looked at Shlomo. "Uh, kid, that's really nice of you, but—just how do you mean to do it?"

Shlomo stood still for a moment, then said determinedly, "We've got nine of us and need only one more. I know two more Jews in this town and I'm going to get one of them to join us!"

"Two more? Who?" Jake was puzzled.

"Who? Jem Fry and his son. That's who. Now you tell the others to wait there on the boat. I'll be right back."

With that, he stormed out of the sheriff's office.

"Jem Fry? Come to the Smuggler's Minyan? Is he out of his mind?"

Simcha and Moshe looked at each other, then at Jake. "You know, I'm really not sure," Moshe laughed.

"Well if he is, so am I," Simcha said. "Cause I'm going after him."

Simcha and Moshe raced out after Shlomo into the darkening day.

## Rejection

Once again the three young men stood on the steps of the beautiful wooden house. Once again Shlomo rang the bell, long and loud. Once again the door was opened, this time by the young man, the banker's son. He was dressed in designer jeans, a light yellow Izod shirt, and was wearing moccasins without socks.

"Yes?" he said, somewhat taken aback by the unexpected visitors.

"Could we come in for a moment? We'd like to talk with you. It's very important," Shlomo said.

Not for the first time that day, Simcha found himself surprised at the way Shlomo had taken charge. His friend—yes, he admitted, his friend!—was changing. Just as the Rebbe, undoubtedly, had foreseen.

With a start, he forced his thoughts back from the old apartment house in Brooklyn, to the wooden colonial in the small Georgia town.

"You see, I'm really rather in a hurry," the young man was explaining. He gave a disarming grin. "I promised a friend a sailing lesson."

"Couldn't it wait for about an hour?" Shlomo asked. "We have nine Jews at the synagogue and we need a tenth to complete a *minyan*. We must say *kaddish* for a fellow Jew, whose *yahrzeit* this is. We need you."

"*Kaddish? Minyan? Yahrzeit?* Speak English, man." The boy was growing impatient.

"Don't you know anything about yourself, about your heritage?" Shlomo, too, was losing patience.

Hurriedly Simcha broke in. "You see, Mr. Fry—"

"Bobby," he interjected.

"You see, Bobby, on the day that a person dies—his *yahrzeit*—every year after that, Jews say a special prayer. *Kaddish*, it's called, and it's very important."

"That's nice, but what does it have to do with me?" Bobby looked meaningfully at his watch.

"We can only say this prayer in the presence of ten Jews who have passed *Bar Mitzvah* age, the age of 13. A *minyan*, it's called. But we've only got nine Jews in The Smuggler's Minyan."

"Oh, the houseboat," Bobby's voice turned wistful. "I used to go there sometimes with my granddad. It was interesting.

Sometimes Isaac Cohen would take me after Grandpa had died."

"Isaac Cohen? Would that be the man called Old Ike, by any chance?"

"Yeah, that's what they called him round here. How did you know?"

"It's Isaac Cohen's *yahrzeit* tonight. It's him we want to say *kaddish* for. It was his last request."

"Old Ike?" Bobby seemed pensive, his former hurry momentarily forgotten. "His last request?" He stopped and thought for a long moment, obviously torn.

Suddenly a flaming red Camaro pulled up. A young man, about Bobby's age, was at the wheel.

"Hey, boy, I thought you were going to meet me on the corner ten minutes ago!"

Bobby shook himself and looked at the young man in the sports car. "One more minute, Jim, okay?"

"Sure, but time's a'wastin'."

He looked at the three boys. "Listen, guys, I'm really sorry, but I promised, see . . ." His words sounded lame, even to his own ears. "Look, what about tomorrow? Can't I join your *minyan* then?"

"Okay, we'll have morning services then," Simcha answered in a reluctant voice. "We'll just have to miss *ma'ariv,* the evening service."

Shlomo's eyes bore into Bobby as he closed the door behind him and made his way to the car. Suddenly Shlomo spoke.

"Tomorrow we won't need you. The men will be here from Savannah. We need you tonight. We came all the way from Brooklyn to be a part of this *minyan.* You, too, must come."

"I'm sorry, I really am." With that, and a wave of his hand, Bobby Fry entered the red car and his friend drove off towards the docks.

There was a moment of complete silence, as the three somberly watched the red sports car drive off.

"Let's see if his father is in," said Shlomo, still determined. He rang the bell again and again and again, in total frustration.

No answer.

Finally Simcha, seeing Shlomo's dejection, put his arm on the other's shoulder and said: "Shlomo, you did all you could. Let's go. They're waiting for us down at the houseboat."

Shlomo flashed a short, grateful smile at his two companions, and the three of them turned around and walked towards the water.

As they walked they felt a wind around them coming in strong gusts. The leaves on the trees shook in a strange and fearful dance; dust began to fly in the superheated air.

They found the houseboat straining at its mooring. Waves leapt against it, moistening the deck. It was something of a feat for them to jump onto the pitching deck, but all three managed without incident.

The boys reported their failure, and some of the older men suggested that they break up for the night and go home. Shlomo, though, demurred.

"Look at the weather out there," he said. "The Fry boy said that he was going sailing. Only a fool would go out on the water tonight. Maybe he'll change his mind and join us for *ma'ariv*. What a shame if the *minyan* breaks up!"

Looking out the portholes the others could not help but agree that it was no night for boating. And so, with Shlomo leading, they recited the afternoon prayers and waited for the coming of evening.

### Hurricane!

The hurricane which hit Pirate's Cove, Georgia, population 890, at 8:07 P.M. on that Wednesday evening was not a very powerful or dangerous one, as hurricanes go. It had flattened some trees in Savannah, overlooked Jessup entirely, and done minimal damage in the outlying towns. It was destined to continue on its southerly path for a few hundred more miles, venting its fury and its power, until it ended up as a typical tropical storm somewhere in Florida. Its final fate was to blow out over the Atlantic Ocean, where it would raise a few waves, frighten a few fish and finally take its last gasp as a blip at a Coast Guard radar station.

No, not a terribly powerful hurricane, as hurricanes go. But to nine people sitting inside a houseboat, it was terrifying.

The nine Jews of Pirate's Cove had talked quietly in the confines of the boat, waiting for evening. They agreed to wait until nine o'clock, and then say the evening prayers, with or without a *minyan*. Old Ike wouldn't have expected them to spend the whole night there, waiting for a tenth Jew.

At 7:59 someone peered out of the dirty porthole and remarked that it seemed awfully quiet out there. The wind, which had been rising all evening, had petered out, and the drenching rain had abruptly stopped. All was still, all but the waves, which grew angrier and angrier with each passing minute. The tide, it seemed would be high tonight.

Abie, the prophet of doom and unfortunate weather phenomena, looked out. The stillness alarmed him. "If anything happens," he commented, "it'll happen pretty soon. Nothin' to do about it now."

And then, some eight minutes later, the wind began to howl and around them pandemonium broke loose!

The waves jumped up twelve, fifteen feet in the air, engulfing the roof of the boat. A fine mist sprayed through the windows and door. The wind, so silent moments before, howled fearfully, its doleful sound reminding Shlomo of the Rosh Hashana shofar. There was a crack of thunder, a bolt of lightning, and the heavens seemed to open. Rain poured down, the waves flew up, all was wetness and water and wind and noise!

"Hurricane!" shouted Abie. "It's come!"

The lights on the houseboat flickered and died out. They sat in blackness.

"What's happened?" Moshe shouted over the din outside.

"Generator! It has an automatic shut-off if too much water gets into it!"

The houseboat, though moored tightly, began to sway back and forth, pitching faster and faster. The benches, fastened down with strong iron bolts, stayed in place, but a few chairs and a table slid wildly across the floor, just missing Simcha's foot.

Then, as suddenly as it had come, the wind, that awful, inescapable, howling and dangerous wind, died down.

"The worst is past," Abie said. "We'll be okay now."

Still, although the worst of the storm had indeed passed on, it left in its wake a torrential downpour, complete with terrible cracks of thunder and awesome lighting bolts. Simcha, witnessing this sight from the safety of the houseboat, murmured the blessing which one makes when G-d's might is revealed. Shlomo followed suit.

One of the younger natives of Pirate's Cove, a denim clad man by the name of Lenny, turned to the three young men, who were riveted to the porthole, fascinated by this blatant display of power.

"Hey, guys, we'd better get that generator working again and check that the mooring is holding. Wouldn't want to find ourselves drifting down in the water would we?"

"Go out? You mean out there?" Moshe, native of a city whose rainy season lasted only a mere four months out of the year, was skeptical.

"Exactly what I mean. It's only raining now. Won't hurt you."

Lenny turned and made his way unsteadily towards the door. Warily Shlomo, Moshe and Simcha followed him. A quick stop at the generator, a flick of a few switches and power was restored. Then the four of them carefully left the interior of the boat.

Although the hurricane was already far away, the rain was heavy. It had grown dark and visibility was almost nonexistent. Lenny grabbed a lantern from a hook, but the spray from the waves quickly extinguished it. He tried to relight it, but his matches were soaked and wouldn't work.

"We'll wait here for a bolt of lightning," he told the soaked boys. "By its light I'll check the mooring. But hold on tight!"

Grabbing hold of the railing on the deck the three boys anxiously waited for the lightning to illuminate the blackness. Suddenly—crack! There it was, a lightning bolt splitting the velvety sky!

Lenny, crouching low near the ropes which tied the houseboat to the dock, nodded with satisfaction. Whoever had tied it up had done his job well—the ropes would hold.

He stood up, ready to tell the wet trio to return to the warmth of the cabin.

"It's okay," he shouted.

Shlomo paid him no heed. "Get me a flashlight," he said urgently.

"What's the matter?" Lenny asked.

"When the lightning bolt appeared, I thought I saw someone out there."

He pointed to the inky blackness of the sea.

"Out there?" Lenny said incredulously. "Impossible. Did either of you see anything?"

Moshe nodded his head; no, he'd seen nothing. But Simcha wasn't as certain.

"I wasn't really looking that way," he said, "but I did notice some movement out of the corner of my eye."

Lenny hesitated, then said: "Well, if there's someone out there, we'd better get a light, and quick." He ran as quickly as he could through the puddles which had gathered on deck, stepped through the door and disappeared. Seconds later he returned, carrying a fresh torch, a lighter and a small pocket flashlight.

"It's not much, but we can't do better," he said. He tried to light the torch once, twice, three times. Finally the wick caught fire, and a small, unsteady flame lit the dark night.

Lenny held the torch near the railing, and slowly moved from one side of the deck to the other. The boys peered anxiously into the sea. Nothing.

"Must have been a piece of driftwood," Shlomo finally said. He turned to return inside when suddenly Moshe called: "One minute. Over there!"

Lenny directed the torch in the direction to which Moshe pointed. Sure enough they saw a head—a tiny, storm-tossed head—wildly bobbing through the water.

"My G-d!" Shlomo shouted. "There's someone out there!"

Lenny, veteran of a hundred ocean storms in his days at Pirate's Cove, did not waste a moment.

"Quick," he commanded, "get a rope. There's one near the door. And a life vest, it's in that corner." He gave the torch to Moshe. "Try to keep him in sight. Lose him and he could go under.".

Simcha dashed down and brought the rope. Lenny quickly tied the life vest, a bright orange one which glowed in the dark, to it. Then, with Moshe trying desperately to keep the bobbing head in sight, he threw the rope with all his might.

"If he's unconscious, he's done for," Lenny muttered. But no! The flailing body seemed to have some control, trying desperately to reach the vest. But it was too far, too far for him to get to.

Lenny, seeing that the person couldn't reach it, pulled in the rope, straining against the waves. Then he threw it again, this time a mighty throw.

Made it! By the light of the torch they could see a person in the water grab onto the vest and try to put it on. His hands slipped, he was under water again! No, this time he'd gotten hold of the vest.

"He's too tired to put it on," Lenny said, half to himself. "We'll have to hope he can hold on so we can haul him in. Boys, I'll need your help."

Pulling a waterlogged rope through heavy breakers is no easy task. Especially when, at the end of that rope, there's a human body.

But when a human life is at stake, the impossible sometimes occurs.

The four of them pulled. Heaved. Yanked. Slowly, ever so slowly the body clinging desperately to the incongruously cheerful orange life vest was pulled closer.

Finally, with one final pull, the life vest, and the person clinging to it, was hauled onto the deck.

Lenny turned on the pocket flashlight, crouched down, and saw, to his relief, that the young shivering man was conscious and unhurt. He was trying to speak, but instead kept coughing up water.

"It's Jim Boch," Lenny said. "Hold still, Jim, for a minute. You'll be all right."

Again, he tried to speak. "Bobby," he finally wheezed. ". . . out there."

"Bobby? Bobby Fry? Where is he?" Lenny asked urgently. "Was he with you?"

The boy took a deep breath, coughed again and then seemed to feel better. "Yes," he whispered in a shivering voice. "Our boat . . . capsized . . . Skull Rock . . . pinned under the mast . . . can't swim . . ."

"Jim, did you say that Bobby is pinned under the boat?"

The boy nodded.

"When you last saw him, was he alive?"

He nodded again.

"Where is Skull Rock?" asked Moshe.

"It's only around fifty feet from here," Lenny answered. "Ordinarily, you could swim there in minutes. But now, with the breakers and the darkness . . ."

"Give me that vest," Moshe demanded, his hands trying to loosen the vest's water-swollen knots.

"Wait a minute! You can't go out there!" Lenny protested.

"I can't let him drown, either!" Moshe continued. "Don't worry, I've got a lifesaving certificate and I'm a strong swimmer."

There! The knot loosened. He took off his windbreaker and donned the vest.

"Where did you say Skull Rock was?" he asked again. His tone of voice was so commanding, that Lenny could only point to the right. "Five minute swim? No problem."

Without another word, Moshe took his wallet from his pocket and handed it to Simcha. Then he took off his *yarmulke*,[22] stuffed it in his pocket and leapt off the railing into the murky waters.

Simcha, astounded, stood in the rain watching his friend swim in the dark frightening-looking water. Then he turned to Lenny. "Do you have another vest?" he demanded.

Lenny silently pointed to the corner of the deck, where a stack of life vests were piled up.

Muttering the words of the *Shema*,[23] Simcha also stuck his *yarmulke* into his pocket and strapped the vest to his back. Then he handed Lenny his and Moshe's wallet and leapt into the water after his friend.

Shlomo, left with the dumbfounded Lenny, stood frozen,

[22] *yarmulke*—skullcap.
[23] *Shema*—A special prayer.

staring at the wild, dark water. He could make out two dots of orange bobbing in the water.

"He went in," Shlomo muttered quietly. "He went in after his friend."

He stood still for a moment, and then, with a decided shrug of his shoulders, raced to the vests lying in the corner.

Lenny, who'd regained some of his composure, tried to stop him, but Shlomo just handed him his wallet, took off his black jacket and *yarmulke* and jumped into the water.

Lenny followed with his eyes the progress of the three bobbing dots of orange in the rainy, rough water.

"Will . . . they . . . get to him?" the half-drowned man whispered.

"I don't know," Lenny replied slowly. "But fella, if you can, you'd better pray."

# CHAPTER 11
## Tamari Takes a Trip

*P*roblems. Nothing but problems. If Colonel Tamari had been a bit more dramatic, he would have torn his hair out. Instead, he lit yet another cigarette.

Problems. A case in Europe that wasn't going well. One of his best agents retiring and no replacement in sight. A construction worker on a project in the neighborhood coming in with some sort of garbled tale of a man on a scaffolding with binoculars. Nothing but troublesome, annoying problems.

Face it, Tamari, he thought to himself, nothing here is unusual, all the problems are routine. Be honest with yourself—you know what's bothering you.

His eyes turned to the framed color photograph on his desk, a picture of a young handsome boy in jeans and a t-shirt.

Impatiently, he banged a button on his desk, and barked through the intercom: "Ella, is Mrs. Stern here yet?"

Ella, his secretary, spoke, laughter in her voice. "Yes, Colonel. She came in a few minutes ago."

"A few minutes ago! Why didn't you tell me?"

"You gave orders not to be disturbed, sir."

So he had. Irritated with himself, with Ella, and with the world, he told Ella to let Mrs. Stern in. He rose from his chair to greet Mrs. Stern.

"Shalom, Shulamis. How's your grandson doing?"

"Thank God, he's much better. They hope to let him out of the hospital next week. He'll need to convalesce, of course, but he should be fine in a few months." Mrs. Stern paused, looking intently at Tamari's anxious face. "But Asher, what's on your mind? You didn't drag me away from Yosef's bedside in order to ask me polite questions."

"You're right, I didn't. Shula, I want to know exactly what you told the boys about Yehuda Bar Eliav."

"Yehuda?" Mrs. Stern seemed genuinely surprised. "You're still worrying about that? I thought he was dead and gone and it was all a wild goose chase. Besides, I told you, the boys won't go looking without me."

Colonel Tamari looked at her shrewdly. "You know the boys. Are you certain of that?"

Shulamis Stern grew sober for a moment, then brightened. "There's really no reason to worry, Asher. The Goldmans would never permit them to go to Georgia by themselves. Simcha told me that himself. If you're really so nervous, though, why not call the Goldmans and make sure the boys are all right?"

Why not, indeed? The truth was, Colonel Tamari hated to think of himself as a worrying father, one who kept checking up on his son. Moshe was bright, resourceful, and independent. And yet . . . somehow, through no fault of their own, they'd gotten involved with the Bar Eliav case. At this point, if they managed somehow to track down Bar Eliav's whereabouts . . . well, things could get dangerous.

Tamari picked up his telephone receiver, dialed the international code.

After a short phone conversation with Mrs. Goldman, the worried look on his face grew more pronounced.

"They've gone to Georgia," he told Mrs. Stern sharply. "Now, who knows what they'll find."

"I still don't understand what all the fuss is about," Mrs. Stern said a little uneasily, but Colonel Tamari wasn't listening. He sat, lost in thought for a minute and then buzzed his secretary.

"Ella," he said, "book me on the next direct flight to New York. Then let me know what time I'm leaving."

"Asher," Mrs. Stern said, startled. "Do you really think the boys are in danger?"

Colonel Tamari was red with anger and didn't answer for fear of putting his foot in his mouth. Until the boys were safe, he felt it was wise not to confront Mrs. Stern.

"Look, let me know what's happening. I'll be in Haifa if you need me."

Mrs. Stern took her leave. But instead of returning to the bus station to board a bus for Haifa, as she planned, she found a phone booth, spoke to someone in the Rambam Hospital and then called her daughter.

The Shulamis Stern, with pursed lips and determined eyes, walked into the office of a Tel Aviv travel agent and inquired about the next direct flight to New York.

# CHAPTER 12
## Churning Waters

$A$lthough he'd been soaked by the rain already, the cold of the sea still came as a shock to Moshe. And the salt water stung his eyes and scratched his throat.

Moshe had battled the treacherous Mediterranean undertow more than once. He was a strong swimmer, a powerful one, but still he was hard put to make any progress through the punishing waves.

Suddenly he felt, rather than saw, a presence coming up behind him. For a moment the thought of sharks chilled him more than the water did.

But he quickly saw it was just another orange vest and the welcome face of his friend Simcha. The lonely, vast dark ocean suddenly did not seem as terrifying anymore.

He raised his hand in mute welcome and pointed in the direction that Lenny had instructed him to go. Together they swam in silence, the sound of crashing waves, pouring rain and dim thunder their only company.

Ten, fifteen long and arduous minutes—minutes that seemed like an eternity—passed. Then they saw it—the outline of a sailboat. Its prow was practically split in half. It had foundered on a large rock—Skull Rock, so named for its strange shape or, perhaps for the many who'd drowned after hitting it.

A bolt of lightning illuminated the area, revealing an eerie tableau—a wrecked, overturned sailboat and, pinned between a fallen mast and the rock, a young man, his body immersed almost up to his neck in the water. But he was alive. He was breathing and he was conscious.

Simcha and Moshe quickly made their way to the desperate young man. Treading water and fighting waves, they tried to pull the mast away, to gain the few inches they needed to free the captive. Bobby watched them, his eyes calm, though frightened.

They pulled and they pulled, and the wooden mast, not built to take the punishment meted out to it by man, by sea, by rock—the mast cracked and came away in their hands. Bobby was free!

Free, but still not out of danger. For with the mast moved away from him, the exhausted boy simply sank into the dark ocean.

Simcha and Moshe searched the water for a sign of him. They cursed the darkness which hampered their rescue efforts. Would all their work be for nothing? Was Bobby Fry, exhausted and possibly injured, destined to sink like a rock into the ocean, just inches away from them?

No! Suddenly they saw him, alive, being hoisted, miraculously, up in the water. Beneath him, to their surprise, was Shlomo, whose orange vest and dripping beard never looked so good!

The three grinned at each other, made a victory sign, and then began the long swim back. They stuck close together with Shlomo half pulling, half carrying Bobby, doing his best to keep his head out of water. Waves broke over them, sometimes carrying them away. Somehow, they struggled back.

Lenny, furious with himself for having allowed the three youngsters to go into the water, held onto the rope, wondering, all the while, if he'd have occasion to use it.

Sooner than he'd thought possible, Lenny saw a flash of orange, no—two flashes, three flashes.

Shlomo signalled to his companions to help tie the waiting rope around Bobby, but Bobby shook his head vigorously. He wanted to pull himself up.

And he did. One, two, three, four soaking wet, exhausted boys climbed up and dropped down on the deck.

Lenny, seeing them all safe, went swiftly into the cabin to tell the anxious men that everyone was safe. Moshe and Simcha followed Lenny, with Shlomo behind, supporting a limping, exhausted-looking, but composed Bobby Fry.

"Well, gentlemen," said Bobby in a low and tired voice, ignoring the twinges in his left leg, "you've got yourself a *minyan*."

## The Rescuers' Reward

After the first startled moment, the men inside The Smuggler's Minyan raced to the assistance of the four wet, shivering youths. Dripping life vests were unbuckled and blankets were found and draped around them. The four drank some fresh water, which soothed throats roughened by the salty sea. Jim was already bundled in a blanket and he and Bobby talked by themselves for a few minutes.

None of them, rescuers and rescued, seemed grievously wounded. Bobby Fry's foot was a bit swollen and gave him some pain, but Doc examined it closely and pronounced it "nothin' worse than a slight sprain—no less than you deserve for havin' gone out in this weather."

Slightly shame-faced, Bobby accepted the rebuke. He'd seen that the weather was strange and might turn nasty, but he'd promised Jim a sail on his boat. He was an expert sailor, and in arrogance, he'd ignored all the warning signs. He'd sure learned his lesson; oh, how he'd learned it!

After they had rested for a few minutes and dried off a bit, Bobby and Jim thanked their rescuers.

"No big deal," Moshe said, embarrassed by their profuse thanks. "Anyone would have done the same thing."

"Don't thank us, it was really not us who saved you—it was G-d Who let us see Jim in the dark ocean," said Shlomo gently.

Bobby ran his fingers through his wet hair in thought. "If I would have listened to you in the first place," Bobby said thoughtfully, "I would have saved myself a sailboat and a lot of grief. Still, you were right—one way or the other, I was meant to be a part of this *minyan*."

And so, having found a *yarmulke* to place on Bobby's wet hair, the Smuggler's Minyan began their evening prayers.

After the prayers, which all aboard said with unusual enthusiasm, Abie glanced outside and announced that it was safe to return home. The wind had died down, the rain had stopped. The hurricane was no more than a bad memory.

"I'd better get back home." Bobby said with sudden urgency. "If Dad finds out that I was on the water, he'll be frantic."

He turned to his rescuers. "Please come home with me. I'd still like to talk to you about so many things. And my dad will also want to thank you for all you've done."

Moshe and Simcha were both ready to refuse because they both felt totally exhausted. To their surprise, Shlomo broke in and accepted the invitation. "We'll stop at the hotel where we're staying first, if you don't mind, to pick up some dry clothing and some of our food."

Doc took them all in his pickup truck. He dropped Jim off home, then brought the boys to their tiny hotel, and finally brought the whole group to the door of the Fry house.

Moshe and Simcha walked towards the door, followed by Shlomo, who was helping the limping Bobby walk. The door was opened, almost immediately after they had rung the door-bell, by a distraught-looking Jem Fry. As soon as he saw the two boys he said: "Haven't I asked you to stop bothering me? What do you want now?"

The banker seemed about to slam the door in their faces, when he caught sight of the limping figure of his son.

"Bobby!" he cried in a voice mixed with panic and relief. "Bobby! Are you all right?"

"Yes, Dad, I'm fine. So is Jim. But the boat . . ."

"Who cares about the boat! Someone told me that they'd seen you go sailing and I've been worried sick about you. I've already had the Coast Guard on the phone and Sheriff Parker . . ."

Suddenly he remembered the presence of the three boys whom he'd almost thrown out of the house moments before.

"You boys . . ." he began.

"They saved us," Bobby broke in. "All three of them. They jumped into the water in the middle of the storm, and almost drowned themselves, trying to save me!"

"They rescued you?" Mr. Fry seemed too moved to speak. "I . . . I don't know what to say."

"What about 'come in, please,' " said Bobby, a little impatient with his father.

"Oh, yes, yes," Mr. Fry led them into the house. The four of them changed into dry clothing, then sat down to talk with the shaken banker. Full explanations followed.

At the end of the narrative, Jem Fry looked at the three youths before him. "I want to apologize for my behavior before," he said, his voice full of feeling. "I was nervous, terrified about my son."

"That's okay," Simcha said sympathetically. "We understand."

"You rescued my Bobby . . ." Mr. Fry continued almost at a loss for words. "I don't know how to thank you."

Shlomo looked up at Mr. Fry with a mischievous grin on his face, "I know how you can thank us, Mr. Fry."

The banker lapsed into silence for a moment, then smiled. "You're right, I do know how to thank you. You and your Smuggler's Minyan . . . Okay, I guess Pirate's Cove will have to have one restaurant less. And perhaps, just perhaps, two more members in its *minyan*. What do you think, Bobby?"

"I think, Dad—that it wouldn't be a bad idea!" replied Bobby, grinning and winking at the boys.

Knowing that Yehuda Bar Eliav was just a trip away, and that the minyan was safe, the three young agents of Emes Junior Interpol went to bed that night, satisfied and content.

The next morning, after a *shacharis*[24] service attended by all the Jews of the Smuggler's Minyan—Jem and Bobby Fry included—and by the four Savannah Jews, who had finally arrived, the three young adventurers prepared to take their leave of Pirate's Cove, Georgia.

Bobby, who still limped a little bit, insisted on accompanying the boys as they said their farewells to their new acquaintances—the sheriff, Jake Gruen, Doc, Lenny and the rest. Then the boys sat together in the cafe, waiting for ol' Abner to come and get them.

"And now," said Simcha, contentedly sipping a Coke, "on to Maine!"

"Maine?" Bobby asked curiously. "I thought you guys were New Yorkers."

They'd forgotten that Bobby knew nothing of what had brought them to Pirate's Cove, and of their discovery of Bar

[24] *shachris*—morning prayer service.

Eliav's whereabouts. They repeated all that they had told everyone else in Pirate's Cove—that they were looking for a friend
who'd been in Pirate's Cove some thirty years back.

In the tradition of Pirate's Cove, the others who'd heard the
story had asked no questions as to why these boys were searching
for someone who had disappeared long before they had been
born. But young Bobby Fry, who lived in Jessup and came down
to Pirate's Cove only for summers, was not schooled in such
reticence.

"Why in heaven's name are you looking for this guy?" he
demanded.

Simcha, Moshe and Shlomo exchanged glances, but none
could see any reason for keeping their task a secret from this boy,
whom they'd come to like in their brief acquaintance with him.
They told all, asking him, of course, to keep the story to himself.

"Spies!" Bobby's eyes lit up. "And the Israeli Shin-Bet! Hey,
you guys are really something."

He popped open another Coke, took a swig, and then asked,
"Listen, fellows, how about letting me join you in Maine?"

He saw their dubious looks and continued:

"Look, I'll tell you the truth. I never knew much about my
being a Jew, never considered it a part of my life. What happened last night showed me I was wrong. I am a Jew. I am part of
the *minyan!*

"But that doesn't help me much, not here. You guys, you
each seem to follow slightly different paths"—this, with a glance
at Shlomo's garb—"but you're Jews, all of you, and you know
what that means. I'd like to learn, to speak with you about all
your different ways. Maybe even choose one of them myself."

"New York is the place for you, then," Shlomo said.

"Or Jerusalem," Moshe added.

"They're right," Simcha concurred. "Running around Maine
is not going to show you much."

Bobby's chin jutted out slightly; he could be stubborn, as stubborn as his father.

"I know that," he said. "But I'm not ready, yet, to commit myself to going to school or anything like that. I'd just like to speak to you guys about Judaism a bit—see what it is I've been missing.

"And," he laughed, "I admit that I've always wanted to do a bit of the cloak-and-dagger stuff myself!" He grew more serious. "But, word of honor, that's not the main reason. I want to speak to you guys, see what makes you tick. What makes you jump into the water for a stranger, or go running around America to look for another Jew."

"Besides," he wheedled, "you might need me. You're going to an island, right? I'm a whiz with boats."

"Yeah, sailboats especially," Simcha teased. But, Bobby knew he had won.

He raced home to get permission from his father and to pack a few things. Shlomo accompanied him, leaving Simcha and Moshe by themselves.

"Well," Simcha said, "that's one job taken care of."

Moshe did not seem to hear him. He was lost in thought.

Simcha looked at him quizzically, and said: "Too bad about that draft notice you got, Moshe. Seems a shame for you to go into the army at your age."

"Yes, it is, isn't it?" Moshe answered absent-mindedly. "Wait a minute!" he said, shaking himself awake. "What're you talking about?"

"Just trying to break through your fog," Simcha smiled good-naturedly. "I got tired of being ignored."

"Sorry. It's just that Bobby's words reminded me of something."

"Huh?"

"An island, Simcha. We're going to an island."

"So what?"

"So—remember the Rebbe's words. Something about the isles rejoicing."

Simcha stood up, and began to gather their luggage. "You know, Moshe," he said, "there's a lot to that Rebbe. He sees a lot, and he knows a lot. Look at Shlomo, and what this trip's done for him already."

"Simcha, do you think—"

"I don't know what I think anymore. But I do know that here comes ol' Abner, to take us to those 'happy isles'.'"

# CHAPTER 13

## The Rejoicing Isle

$A$lthough it was early, the sun was hot, the air still with humidity and dust. Moshe and Simcha could feel beads of sweat form on their foreheads as they piled their luggage onto the battered pickup truck.

"What's keeping them?" Simcha muttered, as he hoisted Shlomo's black suitcase onto the truck. He glanced behind him, but saw no sign of the two.

"A few more minutes and we'll miss that train!" exclaimed Simcha worriedly, looking at his watch for the tenth time.

"Don't worry, you remember Shlomo—goes in for dramatic entrances," Moshe said with a laugh.

Sure enough, not five minutes later, the two boys ran up, panting.

"Come on!" Simcha cried, swinging onto the truck, almost burning his hand on the heated steel back of the pickup. "Not much time left."

"No problem," Bobby told them. He turned to ol' Abner, who had been sitting on a bumper the entire time, chewing tobacco and ignoring the world. "Hey, Abner, give me a hand with these bags."

And to Simcha and Moshe's bafflement, he began to fling the baggage—the baggage they'd just loaded onto the truck—fling it out, onto the ground.

"Are you crazy?" Moshe demanded. "What in the world . . ."

"Not to worry," Bobby assured them. "We're just going first class, is all."

He turned to Abner, apologized for making him wait, and handed him some money. Still chewing tobacco, still ignoring all that was going on, Abner shuffled into his truck and roared away, leaving the four alone in the truck's dusty wake.

"Well, what now?" asked Moshe impatiently.

"Now we wait for my dad. He'll be here in a few minutes. Some details he has to clear up first. Flight plans, that sort of thing."

"Flight plans?" Simcha was confused. "What flight plans?"

"He has to file them. The flight plan from Pirate's Cove to Portland, Maine, with refueling stops along the route."

"Does that mean . . ."

"It certainly does! The bank has a private plane, which Dad is allowed to use for personal use, so long as he reimburses them for gas and things. He's asked a friend of his, a pilot, to do him a favor, and so . . ."

"So we fly to Yehuda Bar Eliav!" Moshe finished triumphantly. Then he sobered up. "But this will cost your father a fortune, won't it?"

"Don't worry, he can afford it. And, to tell the truth he'd like to repay you guys somehow. I know he's promised not to destroy the *minyan,* but he wants to do something for you guys personally as well." He grinned. "For some strange reason he likes me and wants to thank my rescuers."

Moments later Mr. Fry drove up in a large, luxurious beige Chrysler sedan. Their luggage stowed safely in the trunk, the four sat down to enjoy the ride to the local airport.

None of them noticed the small rented car which followed them out. And none of them noticed a swarthy man in the car as he spoke to someone in the airport, someone who had access to the filed flight plans, someone who was willing to sell this information for a few green bills.

And, in the excitement of saying goodbye to Mr. Fry and then the takeoff, no one paid any heed to a small Cessna two-seater which the swarthy man with the large wad of bills had hired for a trip to Maine.

The trip itself passed quickly and pleasantly, even with two refueling stops. The plane was luxuriously appointed, its refrigerator well stocked with fruit and soda. Conversation never flagged, as they spoke to Bobby of Judaism, Israel, *yeshivas*, the Rebbe and, of course, the exploits of Emes Junior Interpol. Bobby was intrigued by all he heard, intrigued and excited and thoughtful.

Although Bobby, veteran of dozens of trips in the small plane, was unexcited about the plane trip, the others felt a thrill of excitement as the plane wove its way through the blue sky. No jumbo jet, this; they could feel every eddy and lurch of the wind, could see the scenery passing below at a speedy clip. Several times during the journey they could hear the roar of a jet passing relatively close to them. Though they could not know it, one of those roars was the noise of an El Al 747 jet. Among its passengers: Colonel Tamari and Shulamis Stern, both bound for New York.

Modern technology can be a wonderful thing. The trip to Maine which, in colonial days, would have taken months; which, in the heyday of the railroad, would have taken days; took a few hours, most of which were spent on the ground, waiting for refueling.

Soon there they were, in Maine, ready to head out to Art's Island.

Inquiries at the Portland airport had borne fruit. It seemed that there were several dozen small islands off the coast, some large enough for whole camps or developments, others tiny enclaves for reclusive millionaires, shy fishermen, or eccentric locals. Art's Island was one of the latter kind, a miniscule dot of an island reached only by ferry, an island containing only one large, old home. The owner? Johnny Doar, businessman, owner of a Manhattan apartment and this, his real home, out on the island.

As they prepared to hail a taxi and drive to the ferry, Simcha hesitated.

"Wait a minute, guys," he said, "don't you think we ought to have a conference first? Sort of decide on a plan of action?"

Moshe, forever the impatient Israeli, disagreed. "What plan of action? It's simple! We go to the island and see if Bar Eliav is there."

"What if he's not? How do we explain barging in on what seems to be a very private piece of property? Besides," Simcha continued, "it seems to me that this may go deeper than we think. Why would Bar Eliav have disappeared, if he's still alive? Maybe he's in on something hush-hush. We might be getting into hot water, barging in and confronting him."

"Simcha's right," Bobby agreed. "We do need an excuse for coming."

"The great Rabbi of Sasov," intoned Shlomo, "once dressed up as a peddler, in order to bring wood to a poor woman."

"So . . ." said Bobby, still unused to Shlomo's way of speaking.

"So," Simcha said, "that's a great idea. We'll pretend to be peddlers . . ."

"Peddlers of Boy Scout cookies!" Bobby ended triumphantly, now that Shlomo's meaning was clear. "We'll pick up some cookies in a grocery . . ."

"Kosher, of course," interjected Simcha.

"Naturally," Bobby said, with a bow. "We'll knock on his

door and try to sell them. Then, we'll try to start a conversation and see if we can get some information."

"I still think you're all spy-happy," Moshe grumbled. "But it can't hurt."

They hopped into a cab, made a stop for cookies and headed out towards the pier. There was one small speedboat moored there, its owner sitting on the wooden pier, napping in the sunshine.

"That must be the ferry to the island," Moshe whispered. "Let's wake up the old guy and get going!"

With some difficulty this was effected. The man stepped into his boat, motioning for the boys to follow.

"Hold on," Simcha said, as Shlomo jumped into the boat. He turned to the ferry driver. "Sir," he said, "when is the next boat out?"

"There's two of us," the man said gruffly. "Other's gone out with a party of picnickers to Marine Island. Should be back in fifteen, twenty minutes, no longer."

"What's the problem?" Bobby asked. "We can all fit in here."

Motioning Shlomo out of the boat, Simcha again called for a quick conference.

"I think we ought to split up. Let two of us wait for the next boat."

There was a chorus of protests. "Why?"

"Just a feeling I have that we shouldn't all rush in together. You remember, Moshe," he said, turning to his partner, "how, whenever we needed advice, we would turn to the *Torah?* And it always came through?"

His friend nodded.

"Well, remember on the train, we were talking about spying and intelligence work in the *Torah?* We mentioned how Yaakov's sons all went into Egypt through different gates, so as not to cause a stir. You yourself called it a smart maneuver. Anyway, I think that we should learn from their example and divide into two groups. Just in case."

Try as he would, though, Simcha could not get the others to agree. Moshe's impatience was contagious and no one wanted to wait for the next boat. They put off all of his arguments and clambered into the boat.

Simcha, though, could be as obstinate as the others. "I'll wait here by myself, then," he insisted. "And I'll meet you in a few minutes."

With a sigh he watched the boat roar off. The pier was quiet and deserted, but there were some buildings further up where he thought he might be able to buy a soda. He glanced at his watch, resolved to return in fifteen minutes, and walked from the pier.

Moments after Simcha had disappeared, another taxi pulled up to the pier. Its one passenger, a swarthy, heavy man, looked at the empty pier in dismay.

"By jet I have travelled," he murmured watching with his binoculars as the small motorboat roared off toward the small island, "and by taxi, boat and train—even by subway! I will not have my journey stymied here!"

He asked the cab driver where he could rent a boat. A ten minute ride, he was told, to a man who hired out speedboats on a daily basis.

"Take me there," the swarthy gentleman commanded. "Make it in five minutes, and there'll be something in it for you."

The taxi driver smiled contentedly to himself, pressed his foot on the gas and they sped off.

The boat speeded through the water, deftly avoiding the weeds cluttering the shore and pulled up to the pier on Art's Island. It was a tiny island, they saw, with the ocean barely visible on the other side, a green island, well-kept and landscaped. In its center on a small rise, near a weeping willow tree, was a large weathered house. "The Doars" announced a small sign swinging in the breeze.

They paid the ferryman and in anxious silence walked up the paved way to the door. Nervously, Moshe rang the bell, then stepped back as the door opened.

He stared at the man who stood in front of him. Forgotten were all the carefully concocted and rehearsed stories which they had agreed upon, for here, without a doubt, standing only inches away was Dagger, otherwise known as Yehuda Bar Eliav, in the flesh!

"Shalom, Mr. Bar Eliav," Moshe said.

The four teenagers who lived in Portland, Maine, had prepared well for their outing. Sandwiches, towels, bathing gear and fishing tackle, all were stowed in their backpacks.

Unfortunately, though, no one had thought to check up on the tide schedules. So, when the ferry which they'd hired pulled up near Marine Island, they saw with dismay that the tide was low, very low. Swimming would be impossible, and fishing difficult.

A hurried conference.

"Let's go to Spooner's Point," a thin brunette with the unlikely name of Pirella suggested. "There's usually good swimming there, even at a low tide."

The others agreed, and the ferryman was instructed to set off again, to Spooner's Point, a ride of another half hour or so.

Simcha glanced at his watch. Fifteen minutes, twenty minutes had passed—where were those ferrymen?

The ferryman who'd brought the other boys to the island decided to put off his return and take a quick trip northward, where the trout, it was said, were bitting fiercely. He thought of the boy who hadn't ridden with him, who had said he'd wait for the next boat. No problem, though—the other boat would be there soon to ferry him down.

He expertly turned his boat and roared on, thinking of the exquisite smell of fried trout.

In a small shack on the water not far from where Simcha waited impatiently, a swarthy man, one who knew something of boating from hours spent on the Volga River, cast off in his hired boat.

# CHAPTER 14
## Bar Eliav's Tale

$T$he tall, dark-haired man with a scar which dominated his facial features, looked keenly at the young man who stood before him.

"Eliav?" he said, with a trace of accent. "I'm sorry, this is the wrong house. My name is Jonathan Doar."

"We know that," Moshe said patiently, though perhaps a little abruptly. "We also know that you used to live in Pirate's Cove, Georgia. My friend, here," he pointed to Bobby, "is a native of that town. My other friend," he continued, pointing to Shlomo, "comes from a small neighborhood in Brooklyn, one in which you used to frequent. He is an emissary of a man known as the Reb."

Doar, or Bar Eliav, seemed visibly staggered by the mention of the Reb.

"Come in," he said. "I think that we had better talk."

The boys followed him into a living room whose furniture bespoke quiet elegance and comfort. In one corner sat an elderly man reading what appeared to be a technical journal.

Bar Eliav ignored the man, and did not introduce him. Instead, he said to the boys: "What, exactly, brings you here?"

"Well, Mr. Bar Eliav . . ." Moshe began eagerly.

The man shook his head. "Doar, I said. Jonathan Doar."

"Mr. Doar," Moshe said, "it all began with a friend of ours, a Mrs. Stern."

"Shulamis Stern?"

"Yes, Mrs. Stern has done some work for my father, whom I believe you know. Colonel Tamari. He told her that she could try to find you, for she'd never believed that you were dead."

"Tamari did that?" Doar was incredulous, but seemed to have finally dropped the pose of not knowing anything of what they were talking about. "Impossible!"

"Well, that's what Mrs. Stern told us. But when she had to unexpectedly return to Israel we went to the Reb, and . . ."

Slowly Bar Eliav drew the tale out of Moshe. At the end he sighed, smiled, and said: "Well, it looks like you boys are worthy of your name—Emes Junior Interpol. You sure tracked me down!"

Shlomo looked at him and spoke for the first time. "The question now, Mr. Bar Eliav, is—did you want to be found?"

Bar Eliav sighed again. "Did I want to be found? Who knows? Sit down, boys, and I'll tell you a story, then, perhaps, you will decide for yourselves."

"I was born," Bar Eliav began, "in Russia, at the end of the first World War. My parents, though Jewish, had nothing left of their Jewish tradition. They were socialists, ardent ones, who lost their lives during the upheavals following the Russian Revolution. I was left to fend for myself.

"I was doing fairly well, and had been accepted to university on a scholarship. Then came the German onslaught. They took over my city and began to round up Jews. I fled, joining a group of partisans in the woods. We were idealistic, but inexperienced. Soon most were killed or captured. They captured me, but I escaped. It was then the Germans gave me this present."

He pointed to his scar.

"I joined another band, a more battle-hardened one. We did great damage to the German cause—blowing up bridges, rail ties, sometimes even army camps. I told no one of my origins. It was not that I kept it a secret, it just never seemed important to discuss.

"Slowly I began to take a position of importance in the group. My fluency in several languages was invaluable, as was my knowledge of bombs. When the leader of the band was killed, I took his place. Dagger, they called me, for I liked my strikes to be swift and brutal."

Bar Eliav's words, at first hesitant, now came out swiftly, as if the torrent which he'd dammed up behind a wall of silence was now coming out. The three young men listened, spellbound.

"And so it went," he continued, "for some years. In 1944 it was obvious that the Germans were on the run. Still we fought, hoping to hasten their defeat.

"One day our band came upon a young couple with a child hiding in the woods. They were nearly starved, and they pleaded with us for food and the chance to join us. They were Jews who had somehow escaped deportation.

"'Jews,' said one of my close comrades in disgust when he saw them, 'be gone with you. These are our woods. You're lucky we're nice enough to let you live and not try to finish the one job that the Germans have done well.'

"He brandished a gun and the family staggered away.

"I was startled, shocked, humiliated. We talked little in those woods, but we made strong, lasting friendships. Or so I thought.

"I said nothing and went back to the camp with the others. But the thought haunted me—I am a Jew, too. It could have been me there, or my sister, whom I'd lost track of.

"As I have said, my Jewishness had not meant much to me. But it was only then, when confronted with the blatant anti-semitism of my comrades that I realized that I was a Jew, *not* a Russian. Strange as it seems, sometimes it takes blind hatred and prejudice and evil to bring one to the truth.

"That night, after much soul searching, I left my band. I came upon the young couple. Their child was ill, desperately ill. I helped them nurse it back to health and gave them food. Then I did something strange—something I would have never believed I could do. I promised to lead them to escape—to Palestine.

"Palestine, like my Jewishness, had meant little to me, but now it seemed as if I had to get out of Russia, as if the very air despised me. These young people—who, incidently, were religious—taught me much about my religion, and about the land which I came to love, even before I reached it.

"To make a long story short, I arrived in Palestine safely with them—I believe they live in Jerusalem now—and I joined the Irgun. It was there I met Shulamis Stern and Asher Tamari.

"But, to be honest, the years had taken their toll. I was tired of fighting, and killing, and bombing. So, a few years later, when someone was needed to go to America for ships and arms, I volunteered.

"I was given a passport and a new identity, that of a Chassid. In Brooklyn I met the Rebbe, and I was really quite impressed with him. But, I had a job to do, and thus could not afford to stay and learn from him.

"I discarded the guise of Chassid and took still another passport. The name—Jonathan Doar, American citizen.

"As this Doar, I contacted several persons of dubious repute about the possibility of procuring arms. Remember, all had to be done illegally. I was promised a fully outfitted ship, complete with arms. I was to pick it up in a small harbor in Georgia. Pirate's Cove it was called. I was to bring the payment, in small bills, with me.

"But, when you deal with crooks, you must be prepared to

be robbed. On the waterfront I was double-crossed. The boat, it appears, did not even exist! They had swindled me, hoping to get my money. They hit me on the head, grabbed the cash, and left me for dead.

"Luckily," Bar Eliav smiled, breaking the tension, "I've got a hard head. Some days later, I found myself in the strangest hospital I'd ever seen."

"Mobley's Saloon and Hospital!" interrupted Bobby and Moshe nearly in unison.

"That's right," said Bar Eliav, a little surprised that they knew of this strange hospital. But then he recalled that they'd said that they just returned from Pirate's Cove. "Anyway, a man called Doc nursed me back to health. Didn't ask many questions, but that seemed to be the custom in Pirate's Cove. Which was lucky for me. You see, if he'd asked me a lot he'd have found that I didn't know anything about myself! I remembered the seven or eight languages which I spoke; I remembered every detail of how to assemble a bomb. But I did not, could not remember my name, my address, where I'd come from, or what I was even doing in Georgia!"

"Amnesia!" exclaimed Bobby.

Bar Eliav nodded. "That's right. It was, I assume, partially physical, a result of the blow I'd received, and partially psychological—I had, you remember, been wanting to break off with my violent past.

"But I said nothing. The habits of a partisan resistance fighter—absolute silence and secrecy—die hard. I didn't let on that my past was a dim shadow. I had a name, a passport, and a little money in my pocket.

"I made my way to Jessup, the nearest city. There my knowledge of languages served me well. I got a job, made some money, managed to buy myself some more identity papers—not difficult for an ex-spy—and finally began a successful import-export house. I travelled often to Russia, particularly, but no one paid heed to the American citizen who came on business.

"I married a lovely woman—Jewish, by the way, which I suppose was instinctive. We had no children and she passed away last year."

He was silent for a long moment, his forehead creased in thought.

"When did you remember who you were?" inquired Moshe gently.

"The psyche is a strange thing. There I was, a prominent businessman in Jessup, happily married and settled. I had heard, of course, of the founding of the Jewish state—one couldn't miss the news about tiny Israel—but it meant little to me.

"Suddenly, in 1965, the Shin-Bet was in the news again. An Israeli spy, one Eli Cohen, had been uncovered in Syria, and was to be hanged. In one of the background stories there was a picture of an old comrade of mine, who'd joined the intelligence agency.

"I don't know why it happened, but that picture did what nothing else had done. It pierced through my amnesia and my entire past came back to me!

"Well, what was I to do? Return to Israel? Leave Jessup, my business, my wife, and return to a country where I had lived for only a short time? The Irgun was disbanded, so I didn't even have an organization to join. Besides, I was older and unused to a life of violence.

"So I stayed on. I was Jonathan Doar, businessman. I did leave Jessup—for some reason, I didn't feel comfortable there anymore, knowing that I had inadvertently deceived my friends for all those years. Before I left I sent a postcard to the Rebbe, for I felt sure he had been anxious about me."

"He was," Moshe assured him. "He hung onto that post-card—which, by the way, you mailed from Pirate's Cove."

"Yes, I had a summer home there. When I left Jessup, I moved to this island where I now live most of the time. I have an office and an apartment in Manhattan, too, but I enjoy the solitude of the island, particularly now that my wife is gone.

"And that is my story. Now tell me—am I glad to have been discovered?"

The boys had no chance to answer, for at that very moment a swarthy man burst into the room.

"Don't move, anyone!" he shouted.

Moshe saw, in silent shock, that in his hand was a short, vicious looking gun.

## Under the Gun

"Okay," the man barked. "To the wall, all of you."

The three boys, Bar Eliav and the elderly man cautiously backed up towards one wall, their eyes on the black, shiny revolver.

The man frisked them, beginning with the boys. Bobby felt a curious urge to giggle, but suppressed it. It all seemed so fake, like something out of a bad movie. Only that gun gave the scene its grim sense of reality.

The boys, of course, had no firearms, but they were somewhat surprised to see the man pull a small revolver from Bar Eliav's pocket.

Then he approached the elderly man.

"From you, Professor, I expect no guns," the man said. "So please, forgive me." With unusual solicitude he searched the man.

He then pulled the elderly man by the arm and walked towards the telephone. He placed one hand, still holding the revolver, next to the old man's head.

"One false move," he warned, "and he gets it!"

Then he dialed a number and began to speak in a foreign language.

The three boys and Bar Eliav, left to themselves, sat down on a couch. They began to whisper, and seeing that this elicited no reaction from the armed man, they turned to Bar Eliav.

"What's going on?" Moshe demanded.

"I—I don't know," Bar Eliav said unconvincingly.

"Oh, come on," protested Bobby. "My dad's a banker, and if there's one thing he's taught me, it's how to smell a put-on miles away, and brother, this is some put on! Mr. Doar—Bar Eliav, I think that your story sounds a bit fishy. I think there's something you're not telling us. Now that we're being threatened by this lunatic, the least you can do is let us know what's happening."

Bar Eliav thought for a minute, then slowly, and in a near whisper so the swarthy man wouldn't hear him, he began to talk. "Okay. But you are wrong—the story is true—only the ending isn't. You see, when I regained my memory, I tried at first to ignore my origins and my adopted homeland, but I found that I couldn't. I felt a strong sense of loyalty to Israel, to Jews. By a strange quirk of fate I had done nothing for my people or my land for many years, but I couldn't continue to live as a contented American citizen.

"So, after revealing the truth to my wife and speaking with her, I decided to do what I had to do. I wouldn't give up my way of life—that wouldn't be fair either to my wife, or to myself— but I would do whatever I could for Israel. And, in my position as an American businessman with many contacts in the Communist world, that could be quite a lot.

"I contacted some old Irgun comrades quietly, clandestinely. I offered my services, to be used only rarely, in times of extreme need. I had impeccable credentials and background. I would be a super-secret agent of the Shin-Bet!"

Here Bar Eliav quickly glanced at the swarthy man, who was

still speaking on the phone, gesticulating wildly. The elderly man stood next to him, calm and unafraid.

He lowered his voice even more, so that the boys had to bend in to hear him. "Only two or three people in Israel knew of my existence, and of whom I had been before and what I was now. My contact in Israel, my boss, so to speak, was Colonel Asher Tamari."

Moshe drew in a deep breath. "*Abba!*"[25]

"That's right," Bar Eliav nodded. "Shulamis Stern was unaware of what had happened. That's why I'm certain that this was a mistake. Your father would never have sent her to find me! He knew where I was. Keeping my whereabouts a secret was his main goal!"

"Mrs. Stern didn't exactly say he'd sent her . . ." said Moshe thoughtfully.

"It sounds like Shulamis hasn't changed much," Bar Eliav said with a hint of a smile. "Probably something set her on the track, and there was no stopping her!"

"But what's going on now?" Bobby said impatiently. "Who are these people?"

"The mad Russian, as I presume him to be, I don't know. The other man, though, is Professor Misha Kardof—one of the most prominent atomic scientists in Russia. Like myself, he was totally dedicated to Russia until he discovered that the modern Soviets, like the Soviets of the 1940's, do not especially like Jews, and they only tolerate those who are needed. Like me, he turned to Israel, wishing to defect. I was in Russia at the time, on business, and so I took care of it. He's been with me, waiting for debriefing and recovering from his ordeal. Later, when the heat dies down, he was to be brought to Israel."

The Russian finally hung up the phone. Still holding his gun

[25] *Abba*—Hebrew for father.

firmly in the small of the elderly man's back, he walked towards the seated group.

He could not keep the triumph out of his voice.

"Well, I have tracked you down!" he gloated.

Bar Eliav saw no reason for pretense. "Yes, it appears you have," he answered mildly. "May I ask how you managed that feat?"

In victory, Yuri could afford to be generous with explanations. Besides, he couldn't resist displaying his own prowess and ability.

"No problem," he said grandly. "I merely followed Courier—you've heard of Courier, no doubt!"

"Courier?" Bar Eliav was shocked. "Impossible. Courier never came here. A change in plan. He was to arrive next week."

"What do you mean, impossible? How do you think I found you? I followed that miserable woman, who thought she could lose me in the foul subways of New York!"

"Woman?" Bar Eliav was puzzled, and then the light of comprehension dawned in his eyes. "Oh! You thought—you thought that Mrs. Stern was Courier!"

"Of course she was!" Yuri's assurance broke down for a moment, but then he regained his composure. "Even if she wasn't—she led me to you and to our honored professor." He turned to the boys. "Yes, gentlemen, how does it feel to know that you led me to this defector? But," he said, with a bow to the old man, "you will be a defector no longer. You'll be glad to know, Professor, that we will soon be meeting a submarine which will give you a free ride back to our motherland. Our own journey," he glanced at his watch, "begins in one half hour. And now, I leave you gentlemen. See to it that you make no move or the professor will, as you say in your language, 'get it.'"

He led the professor into the kitchen to ask him some questions and sat holding the gun pointed steadily at his head.

The others, left alone, lapsed into depressed silence.

"Hold on!" Bobby whispered, after a few minutes. "We've forgotten about Simcha!"

"Who?" Bar Eliav asked.

"Our friend. He refused to come with us, said there might be trouble and we should split up. He was smarter than we were, I guess. He should be here any minute.

"Terrific," Bar Eliav said. "He knocks, walks into a trap, and the Russky has got himself another prisoner."

Silence again. The four of them desperately tried to think of a way out of their predicament.

Moshe's eyes roved around the room. Perhaps he could find a weapon . . . Nothing. His eyes rested for a moment on his new friend, Bobby Fry, on his jeans and jacket and red bandanna . . . his red bandanna . . .

He almost shouted in triumph, but remembering the Russian sitting close by, he restrained himself and whispered: "I've got it!"

"Got what?" Bobby asked.

"Shlomo, do you remember when we spoke about spies in the *Torah*?"

"Yes. That's what gave Simcha his bright idea."

"Well, it's just given me my bright idea. The spies, Shlomo—they were helped by a woman named Rachav, who lived in Jericho. Right? The spies promised that her household wouldn't be harmed when the Jews came into the city, right? And how did they mark her house? They tied a red cloth to the house, that's how. Red cloth," he ended, looking significantly at Bobby's neck.

Bar Eliav caught on. "And you think if we tie that scarf to the window, your friend will see it and realize that—"

"That something's wrong!" Moshe said excitedly. "Yes, I'm sure of it. I know Simcha—he's sharp. He'll know."

"So now the problem is getting this bandanna out there."
Bobby had already stripped off his bright red scarf.

Bar Eliav glanced up and saw that the Russian had once again
picked up the phone.

"That should keep him busy for a few moments," he muttered.

Slowly, ever so slowly, Bar Eliav edged his way to the end of
the couch, and then stood up. The Russian, occupied on the
phone, noticed nothing. In total silence Bar Eliav made his way
to the small window which was closest to him.

He'd made it. Cramming the bandanna into a pocket he
raised the window an inch, three inches—enough! Swiftly he
took the bandanna out and tied it around one of the bars which
covered the window.

The Russian replaced the phone onto the receiver, turned
around, and saw him.

"What are you doing?" he barked, waving his gun menac-
ingly.

"Nothing, nothing," Bar Eliav said, his back to the Russian.
"Just trying to open this window. We need some fresh air."

He turned to face them, and with relief the others saw that the
bandanna was not in his hand. He'd done it!

"Well close it!" the Russian commanded. "And stay seated,
all of you."

With a careless shrug, Bar Eliav closed the window and drew
the curtains, thus ensuring that the Russian would not notice the
red scarf flying in front of the house.

"Now we have to sit and wait, and hope that your friend
comes through," Bar Eliav said quietly.

Moshe spoke in total confidence. "Don't worry," he said,
"he'll come through."

# CHAPTER 15
## Simcha Hires a Boat

Simcha Goldman was hot. And bored. And frustrated.

For the thousandth time he scanned the blue water, searching for a dot, a telltale wake or wisp of smoke—anything, any sign of the ferry.

Nothing but minnows, mindless of his sorrows.

Why, oh why, did he have to be so cautious all the time? The others had undoubtedly discovered their man, and he was missing all the excitement, sitting on this lonely pier.

Not knowing what else to do, he trudged back up the road and flagged down a passing car.

"Is there any other way of getting to Art's Island?" he asked the driver, a genial looking middle aged fellow.

"Boat rental down that-a-way," he answered, pointing straight ahead. "Few minutes drive from here. Want to hop in?"

He turned around, looked again at the empty sea. No, he couldn't face another minute of this endless waiting. "Sure," he said, climbing in.

Simcha had gone boating a few times on placid lakes during summer vacations. But he had never taken a speedboat on the ocean, and thus it was with some qualms that he signed the papers and prepared to strike out to sea.

The instructions seemed clear enough. Art's Island, the boat-man had said, was almost exactly straight ahead, and impossible to miss.

Impossible to miss is right, Simcha thought, a few minutes later. He had almost crashed right onto it! At the very last moment he had remembered to shut off the motor, and he'd drifted onto the beach, not far from the pier which had been his destination.

"Not bad for a landlubber," he thought, regarding the beach, the boat, and the wooden house in front of him with satisfaction. He'd made it!

He started up the walk and in his preoccupation took no notice of the red scarf flying in the wind. He picked up the ornate brass knocker, prepared to let it down.

Suddenly he noticed the red scarf tied to a bar in front of one of the windows.

Gently he let down the knocker and walked over to the red cloth. It looked faintly familiar. In fact, it looked like the ban-danna Bobby had been wearing. But why here?

Moshe had often berated Simcha for what he considered excessive caution. It was this caution that now made Simcha hesi-tate for a moment and not return to the door.

Why Bobby's scarf? Why here?

Red hanging on a building. It reminded him of something. Of . . . of . . . Rachav and the spies! But what did it all mean?

A sign? Was it a sign? To leave this house alone, perhaps?

Pursing his lips in thought he quietly walked away from the house and circled around the back.

He didn't know what he expected to see. Certainly not the sight which lay before him as he peered into a kitchen window. There was a tall man carefully tying up his three friends and a short, swarthy man—who in a shock of recognition Simcha realized was the weird man from the Empire State Building elevator! A closer look revealed that this man was holding a gun on an elderly man!

He quickly stepped back from the window, so that he would not be sighted by those inside. A sign, indeed! His friends needed help!

But so did he.

He hated to leave them, but he quickly turned and raced back to his speedboat. He knew he could do nothing by himself, not against a man with a menacing revolver. If he burst in someone might be hurt, even killed, before he could do a thing.

He gunned the motor and raced the boat as it had never been raced before!

Faster than he thought possible he was back at the boat rental. Astonished at the expertness with which he moored the boat, he ran inside.

"Help! I need help! My friends are on Art's Island and there's a guy there holding a gun on them!"

It sounded crazy, even to his own ears. The owner of the boat, a skeptical Yankee of six generations, smiled.

"That's too bad. A man with a gun, huh? What is this—it's too warm to be an April Fool's joke—"

Simcha impatiently interrupted.

"Sir, I know it sounds strange, but it's true. My friends are in Jonathan Doar's house and I looked inside and saw that they were being held prisoners. I need help!"

"No, it's not April Fools. It must be a fraternity initiation! Yeah, you boys get more original every year."

Still chuckling, the man left Simcha and walked into his kitchen to brew himself a coffee.

Simcha was in a quandary. He could try the police, but would they believe him? The odds were against it. By the time he'd convince them of his seriousness, of his sanity, his friends might be . . . no, he wouldn't think of that.

Grimly he walked back to the boat, jumped in and turned on the motor. He would save his friends—or share their fate!

The skeptical Yankee watched him go. "These kids today!" he chuckled, sipping the steaming brew from his mug.

## Rescue

The dark Russian examined the bonds which Bar Eliav had just tied around the three boys' hands and feet.

"Very good," he said approvingly. "You are a seaman, I see."

He pointed to the professor, who had not yet uttered a word. "Now, my good man, please tie up our distinguished friend. Just his hands, please, for he will have to walk with me to my boat."

Bar Eliav took another piece of rope from the kitchen (solid nautical rope, to be used for his boat,) and, seeing no alternative, he tied the professor's hands. Yuri carefully examined the knots.

"Now," he said, "you leave me something of a problem. I need both hands to tie you up, but I must keep one on my revolver. So . . ."

Without warning he whirled on Bar Eliav and brought the gun butt down on his head. The man collapsed in a heap.

"I suppose you will, eventually, get out of your bonds," Yuri continued. "But I will buy myself a bit more time, by doing this—" and he grandly ripped the telephone cord out of the wall, "and by availing myself of Mr. Doar's oh-so-lovely speedboat I noticed parked in back."

Yuri appraised his prisoners one last time.

"And now, my friends, farewell. We shall not meet again. Professor, prepare for your homeward journey."

With a final flourish of the gun, Yuri and the hapless prisoner walked out of the house.

Art's Island had two piers, one directly in front of the house, where the boys and the Russian had docked, and one behind the house, which led out to open sea. It was here that Doar had his own speedboat moored.

Yuri walked with the professor to Doar's new sleek speedboat. In his excitement he didn't notice the sound of Simcha's boat approaching. As Yuri roared out, Simcha roared in.

Simcha cautiously circled around the house, carefully peeking into the window. He saw his friends, bound onto chairs; he saw the tall man, lying in a heap on the floor. Of the armed man and the old man, he saw nothing.

He burst inside, prepared for the worst.

"Simcha!" all three cried together.

He raced to his friends and in minutes they were free!

Shlomo raced to Bar Eliav's side. "He's breathing," he reassured them. "I think he's just been knocked unconscious."

"What happened?" Simcha asked breathlessly.

"Never mind explanations," Moshe responded. "How did you get here?"

"Rented a boat, but . . ."

"Is it still here?" Bobby demanded.

"Yes, moored by the pier."

"Then let's go!"

Together they raced out and headed for the boat.

Moshe told Simcha all that had happened as Bobby guided the boat expertly through the water. They were going fast, faster . . . skimming the water, feeling as if they were flying over it and never touching the waves which tossed a soft spray over them.

"Come on, baby," urged Bobby, pushing the motor to still greater speed.

"Are you sure you can handle this, Bobby?" said Moshe uneasily. "We're going very fast—if we capsize, we'll never capture them!"

"Don't worry, I knew how to drive a boat before I could walk!" Bobby assured him, swerving to avoid a rock which seemed to appear out of nowhere.

"Do you see them?" Shlomo asked anxiously.

"Over there," Bobby pointed to a small speck in the distance. "That's them."

The small speck gradually grew larger. Yuri, unaware of the pursuit and not wholly comfortable in the position of speedboater, drove slowly over the water, the still silent professor next to him.

But then Yuri heard something—a putt-putt, a roar of a motor. He took his eyes off the water before him, turned—and there they were! Those troublesome boys again!

Glancing at the rather dilapidated boat which Simcha had rented, and at the ultra-modern speedboat beneath him, he grew calmer. "They will never overtake me," he thought. "And, once we're out in open sea, I will easily lose them."

"Once he's out in open sea," Bobby said, unknowingly echoing his quarry's thoughts, "it'll be impossible to keep him in sight. We've got to get to him now."

He coaxed still more speed out of the straining motor. The speedometer's needle wavered, and then moved into the area marked in red—Danger!

In front of him, Yuri pressed down on the pedal and his boat lurched forward.

Bobby shook his head. "He's getting away from us!" he cried. "I don't know if I can beat that boat!"

Yuri laughed into the wind, sensing the sweet smell of success.

Suddenly an island loomed in front of Yuri. Not a large island, but large enough to force him to slow down and veer to the left.

About two miles down, he saw, the island came to an abrupt end. He would head that way, curve around the tip of the island, and hopefully lose the boys. If not, well, open sea couldn't be much further. His troubles were almost over . . .

So Yuri headed around Spooner's Point.

The band of teenagers from Portland had had no luck that day. First, the bad tide at Marine Island and then, soon after disembarking at Spooner's Point, Joe Macauley stepped on a piece of broken glass. His foot wouldn't stop bleeding, and it looked like he'd need medical attention.

"Let's head back," one of them had suggested in disgust. After some delay, they all climbed into the patient ferryman's boat, and pulled out.

Bobby and the others watched in chagrin as Yuri's boat veered off to avoid the island and slowly approached the island's curved tip. "We're going to lose him," a grim Bobby predicted. "We're going to lose him."

Yuri, just about to turn around the narrow tip of the island, turned around to take one last look at his pursuers. Like them, he was certain that by the time they had edged around the island, he would have reached the vast ocean, where detection would be nearly impossible.

And as Yuri turned around the ferryman carrying the group of teenagers from Portland came around the other side.

The man in the boat rental shack on the mainland heard a faint clap, like a clap of thunder. He looked out at the clear sky, shrugged and forgot about it.

Just regaining consciousness, Yehuda Bar Eliav also heard a clap, and dismissed it as a noise in his own aching head.

In their boat, the boys also heard the clap, and saw Yuri's boat crash into the slow-moving boat of the ferry driver. Three or four bodies hurtled into the air and the two boats sank slowly into the sea.

Swiftly, Bobby navigated the boat as close as possible to the crash and then slowed down so that the others could safely jump out. For the second time in two days, Shlomo, Moshe and Simcha felt the shock of the cold water, as they dove in.

Three of the teenagers, though in shock, were unhurt, and after a moment of confusion they slowly swam towards Simcha's rented boat. Bobby helped them aboard.

Moshe picked up the almost unconscious ferry driver, while Simcha struggled with a teenager whose arm appeared to be broken. Somehow they managed to bring them both to the boat, where the unhurt survivors helped pull them aboard.

Shlomo had raced to the aid of the professor who, unable to use his still bound-up hands, had almost drowned when the boat capsized. Luckily, despite his age, he was still in good shape, and he'd managed to keep his head above water by kicking his legs. Unable to untie the wet ropes, Shlomo heaved the professor over his shoulder and half swam, half floated him to the boat.

And as for Yuri? The erstwhile spy and hero of the mother-land clung desperately to a piece of driftwood from the destroyed ferry.

You see, Yuri, though talented in numerous languages, able to lip-read with ease, had never learned how to swim.

Simcha and Moshe, charter members of Emes Junior Interpol, couldn't help but chuckle as they helped the bedraggled spy to the boat.

# CHAPTER 16
## Explanations

$T$he boys were bone-tired. It was good finally to sit down.

They were back on Art's Island, in the elegant house owned by Jonathan Doar. Doar had an improvised bandage on his head and a look of relief on his face.

After a hasty conference it had been decided that, since the speedboat simply wasn't large enough to travel with everyone all the way to Doar's house, they would ferry the teenagers back, while the others would remain on the nearby island until help could arrive. Bobby took his cargo of teens and wounded ferryman in the boat; the others remained behind to keep a close eye on the swarthy Russian.

Guided by the teenagers, Bobby had brought them to a nearby Coast Guard station. With a cursory explanation—"A collision on the water; I'm going to get the others"—he'd raced off again. He returned to his comrades and their prisoner and then raced off to Bar Eliav's home. They were relieved to find Bar Eliav unhurt and conscious, sitting over a radio transmitter which Yuri had neglected to destroy.

Bar Eliav, just as relieved to see that they'd come to no harm, and ecstatic at the return of the professor, had insisted that they relax on his overstuffed couch, despite their dripping clothing. After they'd rested a bit and told Bar Eliav all that had happened, they went upstairs and changed into robes which Bar Eliav supplied.

Self-conscious in their new garb, which dragged across the floor and covered their fingers, they turned to Bar Eliav.

"What now?" they asked.

"Now, I've got some explaining to do to the local police, who are undoubtedly looking all over for you, trying to find out what happened." He looked at Yuri who sat glum and silent, barely able to move because of the ropes the boys had tied to his hands and feet. "The police here don't exactly take nicely to speeding at sea."

"But don't worry," Bar Eliav assured them, "the chief of police is a good friend of mine. He's on his way here and he should square everything with the law."

With a glance at Moshe, Bar Eliav continued to speak. "This transmitter of mine—a convenient toy—has quite a range. I've spoken with Jerusalem just now and with New York. We should be getting guests quite soon, to take care of the professor and Yuri. Your father, Moshe, should also be here."

"*Abba?*" Moshe said. "From Tel Aviv?"

"No, from Brooklyn. Seems your father suspected that you might be getting into trouble, though I can't imagine why."

"Yes, all we wanted was a quiet boat trip," Simcha said wryly.

"So your father is coming with some other agents—including, by the way, my faithful friend Shulamis Stern, —to take care of everything.

"Until then, we can do nothing but wait. And relax."

With sighs of pleasure, all four did exactly that.

## Brooklyn

Sitting in the quiet atmosphere of the Reb's study, it was difficult for Simcha to believe that the past week's adventures were real.

Yet here they all were—Moshe, Simcha, Shlomo, Bobby, Colonel Tamari, the professor, and Bar Eliav reunited with his faithful friends: Mrs. Stern and the Rebbe.

"Yes, it really was an adventurous week," the Rebbe said. "You boys certainly discovered 'the rejoicing isle'!"

Moshe stared at the venerable man and then asked, with awe in his voice, "Can you really foretell the future, Reb?"

The Rebbe smiled.

"No, prophecy is no longer with us, my son. But there are hints, signs. All can be found in the *Torah,* if only one knows where to look, and how to look."

"And so it all ends, back here in Brooklyn," Mrs. Stern sighed, still quite unable to believe that her quest was complete.

The Rebbe favored them with another shrewd glance. "End? I think not. I think each of the participants have learned, have taken something from this adventure, something which begins just now."

"To befriend and trust and help my fellow Jews," volunteered Shlomo with a grin at the boys.

"To carry no prejudices," Simcha added, smiling back at him.

"And no preconceived notions," concluded Moshe.

"Well, I guess I've also learned something. That it could be dangerous to be so nosy and determined," remarked Mrs. Stern.

Colonel Tamari looked at her sharply, but with affection. "And I guess I've learned that when Shulamis Stern sets her mind to something, she usually manages to get it. In the future, Shula-

mis, I will not dare you to do anything that I don't want you to do. Thank God, this time it's all turned out for the best."

Bobby was quiet for a moment, and then spoke. "All I've learned, I guess, is how little I know, and how much I've got to learn. And, with the Rebbe's permission, I'd like to stay here for a while and catch up."

The Rebbe smiled. "I'm sure we can make your father agree. And Shlomo needs a new study partner, don't you?"

Shlomo's face lit up in eager acceptance.

"What of your future, Yehudale?" the Rebbe asked, looking with concern at Bar Eliav.

"Yehudale. Do you know how long it's been since someone called me that?" mused Bar Eliav. "Me? I spent part of my life in ignorance of my Jewishness, part of my life ignoring it, and part of my life affirming it through violence. Perhaps now it is time to study and practice it—in Jerusalem, where it is practiced best."

Jerusalem.

Simcha and Moshe cast their minds over the miles, to the city of miracles and prayer and ancient walls, to the *Kotel*[26] at dusk and the synagogues on *Shabbat*.[27]

"Are you thinking what I'm thinking?" Moshe asked Simcha.

"Vacations are nice," Moshe answered, "but—"

"But, it's time to go home," Simcha concluded. "It's time for Emes Junior Interpol to head back home."

## The End

[26] *Kotel*—the Western Wall.
[27] *Shabbat*—Saturday, the Jewish day of rest.

# About the Author

Miriam Stark Zakon was born and raised in Brooklyn, New York. She received a traditional Jewish education in the Beth Jacob of Boro Park Yeshiva School for girls and she is a Summa Cum Laude graduate of Brooklyn College and member of the Phi Betta Kappa Honor Society.

Her writing career began in the sixth grade with an underground magazine and since then she has not put her pen down. She is the author of *The Egyptian Star*, the second book in the exciting Emes Junior Interpol mystery series, as well as the translator of *T'zena U'rena*, the classic Yiddish work. She has also written numerous articles in magazines and newspapers in both the United States and in Israel.

She and her husband, Rabbi Nachman Zakon have one son and live in Pennsylvania.

# The Judaica Youth Series
## EMES Junior Interpol
### for ages 12 and up

## THE HOSTAGE TORAH
### The Formation of EMES Junior Interpol
#### By Gershon Winkler
#### Illustrated by Yochanan Jones

A fanatical band of militants have stormed the Israeli Embassy in a small Islamic nation and are holding 34 Jews as hostages. Even the *Shin-Bet*—Israel's crack intelligence team—cannot save them . . .

Until three people cross paths:

MOSHE TAMARI—Son of a *Shin-Bet* officer, and an Israeli exchange student in an American high school. Moshe's eyes are opened when he meets . . .

SIMCHA GOLDMAN—A Brooklyn yeshiva student on vacation in Israel. His learning pays off with a plan . . . but to make it work he needs the help of . . .

JASON SAMUELS—A professor of Anthropology who has spent half his life trying to forget he was Jewish. Jason never makes it to his archeological expedition—he is sidetracked by a series of strange encounters with an aging rabbi, a Palestinian terrorist, and a 3500 year old prophet in the wilderness.

The three team up in this thrilling blend of espionage, suspense, and spiritual confrontation, to plan the daring rescue of the hostages and their escape.

The first of an exciting new series of adventure novelettes for Jewish teenagers ages 12 and up.

5½ x 8½, 128 pages.
Hardbound, $6.95, ISBN: 0-910818-33-9,
Softbound, $5.95, ISBN: 0-910818-34-7

# The Judaica Youth Series
## EMES Junior Interpol
### for ages 12 and up

## The Egyptian Star

### by Miriam Stark Zakon

In this sequel to The Hostage Torah, Moshe Tamari of Israel and Simcha Goldman of Brooklyn, the teenage heroes of Emes Junior Interpol, become involved with a Nazi murderer in Cairo, Arab terrorists and buried treasure. How they deal with the above and explore some basic Jewish values along the way is all part of this exciting adventure-mystery.

Hardbound $6.95 ISBN: 0-910818-47-9
Softbound $5.95 ISBN: 0-910818-48-7

# OTHER JUDAICA PRESS PUBLICATIONS

THE PENTATEUCH (The Five Books Of Moses) — Translation and Commentary by Rabbi Samson Raphael Hirsch, English Translation by Isaac Levi. Six volumes, complete with the text in vocalized Hebrew, the English translation and Hirsch's enlightening commentary.

Student Edition, Six Volumes, 5 x 7½, 3557 pages; $65.00
Popular Edition, Seven Volumes (with Haftaros).
5 x 7½, 4257 pages; $75.00, ISBN: 0-910818-12-6

THE MISHNAH — by Philip Blackman, F.C.S. An annotated translation into English of the most basic text to the Jewish Oral Tradition, upon which the Talmud is based.

Popular Edition, Seven Volumes, 5½ x 8½, 4050 pages; $75.00
Student Edition, Six Volumes, 5½ x 8½, 3676 pages; $65.00
Presentation (Leather) Edition, Seven Volumes, 6 x 9, 4050 pages; $150.00
ISBN: 0-910818-00-2

DYBBUK — by Gershon Winkler, illustrated by Yochanan Jones. A Selection of six documented accounts of soul-possession and exorcism in the Jewish Experience, the dybbuks of Safed, Smyrna, Bagdad, Brisk and Radun; dramatically adapted for the contemporary American reader.

6 x 9, 368 pages;
Hardbound, $13.95, ISBN: 0-910818-38-x
Softbound, $9.95, ISBN: 0-910818-37-1

MAIMONIDES' INTRODUCTION TO THE TALMUD — by Zvi Lampel. The original text of Maimonides' monumental aid to the understanding of the talmudic structure and tradition, translated into a flowing English rendition which won the book the *Jewish Book Council Award*.

6 x 9, 296 pages; $7.95, ISBN: 0-910818-06-1

THE JASTROW DICTIONARY — by Dr. Marcus Jastrow. A definitive dictionary on the Babylonian and Jerusalem Talmuds, the Targumim and Midrashic literature.

One-Volume Compact Edition, 5 x 7½, 1736 pages; $19.95
ISBN: 0-910818-05-3

# OTHER JUDAICA PRESS PUBLICATIONS

HALACHA — by Yechiel Galas. An invaluable, easy-to-follow guide to daily Jewish practices and special seasonal observances. Also deals with issues of contemporary concern and its treatment by the halacha.

6 x 9, 192 pages, Softbound; $4.95, ISBN: 0-910818-13-4

ANTHOLOGY OF JEWISH MYSTICISM — translated by Raphael Ben Zion. A annotated translation into English of three fundamental kabbalistic texts spanning four centuries: *Tomer Deborah*, *Portal of Unity and Faith*, and *Nefesh Hachayim*.

5 x 7½, 250 pages, Softbound; $6.95, ISBN: 0-910818-29-0

PARDES RIMONIM — by Rabbi Dr. Moshe Tendler. A contemporary halachic and philosophical treatise on marriage, family purity, natural childbirth, population control, genetic engineering, and questions of death.

5½ x 8½, 96 pages, Softbound; $3.95, ISBN: 0-910818-09-6

MIKRAOTH GEDOLOTH (NIVIIM)—the key to fully understanding and appreciating the Books of the Prophets lies in the works of the rabbinical commentators. The definitive Hebrew edition of text plus commentary, the Mikraoth Gedoloth, offers this complete learning experience.

The Judaica Books Of The Prophets Series contains the Hebrew text of the Mikraoth Gedoloth, plus a page of the text in English translation of all Rashis, also Commentary Digest of the classic commentaries and additional sources on the facing pages. Each book of the prophets includes a brief introduction to the central personages in the volume, an outline of major events, a bibliography of the interpretations in the Digest and a map of the geographic areas discussed in the text.

Book of Joshua — 5½ x 8½, 350 pages, $12.95 — ISBN: 0-910818-08-8
Book of Judges — 5½ x 8½, 400 pages, $12.95 — ISBN: 0-910818-17-7
Book of Samuel I — 5½ x 8½, 525 pages, $12.95 — ISBN: 0-910818-07-X
Book of Samuel II — 5½ x 8½, 540 pages, $12.95 — ISBN: 0-910818-11-8
Book of Kings I — 5½ x 8½, 512 pages, $12.95 — ISBN: 0-910818-30-4
Book of Kings II — 5½ x 8½, 480 pages, $12.95 — ISBN: 0-910818-31-2
Book of Isaiah (Vol. 1) — 5½ x 8½, 520 pages, $12.95 — ISBN: 0-910818-50-9
Book of Isaiah (Vol. 2) — 5½ x 8½, 610 pages, $12.95 — ISBN: 0-910818-52-5
Book of Jeremiah (Vol. 1) — 5½ x 8½, 480 pages, $12.95 — ISBN: 0-910818-59-2
Book of Jeremiah (Vol. 2) — 5½ x 8½, 464 pages, $12.95 — ISBN: 0-910818-60-6